The Night Boat

The Night Boat

M.J. Todd

This is a work of fiction. Names, characters, places, and incidents either are the product of the author's imagination or are used fictitiously. Any resemblance to actual persons, living or dead, events, or locales is purely coincidental.

Copyright © 2022 by Martin Toddington (M.J. Todd)

All rights reserved. No part of this book may be reproduced by any means or used in any manner without written permission of the copyright owner except for the use of quotations in a book review.

Book design by M.J. Todd

Contents

Chapter 1 1
Chapter 2 11
Chapter 3 17
Chapter 4 21
Chapter 5 29
Chapter 6 33
Chapter 7 37
Chapter 8 41
Chapter 9 49
Chapter 10 55
Chapter 11 61
Chapter 12 67
Chapter 13 73
Chapter 14 77
Chapter 15 83
Chapter 16 89
Chapter 17 95
Chapter 18 99
Chapter 19 105
Chapter 20 113
Chapter 21 127
Chapter 22 133
Chapter 23 137
Chapter 24 143
ACKNOWLEDGEMENTS 159
Books by M.J. Todd 161

Chapter 1

"Sir...? Sir...? Mr Leadstone, sir...? Would you like a drink?" came a friendly, enquiring voice.

Jeremy Leadstone slowly opened his eyes and saw a blurry figure appear, with a bright aura surrounding it.

"There you are, sir. Would you like a drink?" the polite figure continued.

He winced as he awoke at the intense illumination behind the figure, shielding his eyes as he waited for them to become accustomed to the light.

A young man, smartly dressed in a white smock coat, tanned skin, and a smile came into view. As he focussed on the man, Jeremy recognised the man's uniform and realised that in front of him was a cabin crew member from a cruise ship.

He hoisted himself onto his elbows to scan the area and take in his surroundings, then immediately felt a light stabbing pain in his chest. He was definitely on a ship, and in front of him was a pleasant member of staff asking him if he wanted a drink!

"Where the hell am I?" Jeremy said, as he sat upright, rubbing his chest.

"You're here, sir. On the Pendentes, sir," the waiter smiled with pride. "Don't worry, sir. You are not the first person to wake up and wonder where they are. It happens all the time."

The young man retrieved a small electronic tablet from his jacket pocket and tapped it into life.

"Would you like your usual, sir? Bourbon with ice?" he said, smiling at his disorientated passenger.

Jeremy was still in a daze and struggled to understand what the hell he was doing on a ship, more to the point where he was going.

He noticed, looking around, it was evening time, and the sun had set. The faintest slither of moon appeared over the watery horizon as the ship gently rocked on the nearly non-existent waves, travelling forward to its unknown destination.

Behind Jeremy's new companion was a bright ship's light, which gave him the celestial halo. Looking toward the bow, then to the stern, Jeremy worked out that he was sitting on deck about in the middle of a ship. He figured it was about one hundred metres long. Not an enormous ship, but a ship. He had been on bigger vessels with his wife when they had been on holiday cruises, but could not fathom out how he got there. Where *was* his wife? Where was he going? And when and where did he board?

"Bourbon and ice, sir?" the waiter enquired again.

With a puzzled gaze, Jeremy stared at the young man.

"Who are you? I mean, what's your name and how did I get here?" he asked.

The waiter smiled a strained smile.

"My name is a little difficult to pronounce for some, so they call me Manny. Please, call me Manny. At your service, sir." Manny gave a courteous nod of his head. "You're on the Greek ship, Pendentes. You boarded with the rest of the passengers a short while ago. Anyway sir, evening time approaches, and I thought I'd wake you before it got too late. My mother always said that if you sleep too much now, you'll never be able to sleep at night."

Manny smiled at the nostalgia for his last comment.

Still puzzling over how he got there, another question presented itself to Jeremy.

"This may sound stupid, Manny, but where are we going?"

Manny smiled and stood upright, placing his tablet back into his jacket pocket.

"No, not at all, sir. We'll be docking in a couple of hours. We're travelling south, sir. I'm sure when you fully wake up you'll remember everything, sir."

Manny smiled, nodded his head in respect, and hurried away.

"What the hell?" Jeremy muttered to himself, still not fully awake. "There was no information in that answer at all."

As he looked up into the evening sky, a wonderful deep indigo was replacing the watery turquoise of daytime. The beautiful deepening sky was clear of any clouds, but not a single star was out. Jeremy searched the sky for the North star but couldn't find it.

"Maybe it's too early," he said to himself.

There was an unusual silence in the air. Not unnerving or worry-some, just noticeable.

Jeremy was sitting on the edge of the sun lounger, looking to his right, out to the still waters that sparkled with the moon's rays as they danced on every ripple. As the moon raised itself from behind the horizon, there was something that appeared wrong. It was so minor that his sleepy mind had not yet fully picked up on it.

On his left, he could see another deck above him, with what was probably the captain's bridge at the very top. The ship was immaculately white, and was clearly maintained to an excellent standard, as expected. Below the bridge windows, ornately painted, was the ship's name; 'Pendentes'. Yes, he was definitely on the Pendentes, alright. But how the hell had he got there?

Jeremy wracked his brain but couldn't remember booking the cruise or boarding with his wife, Joanna. He surely hadn't gone on holiday with Lena, a young legal secretary from his law firm, however cute she was. OK, her proportions suited his taste, but she meant nothing to him, so whilst he promised her the world, surely she should have known that nothing would come of it.

He would never leave his wife for some little whore who would open her legs for the boss at the drop of a hat. Especially when the boss was the owner of a highly successful, top law firm, whose clients included some of the wealthiest people in the country.

He wasn't stupid. Not at all. He was everything he wanted to be. Standing over 6-foot-tall, he possessed a full head of dark, expensively cut, combed back hair. Jeremy was good for someone of his age and had a physique a 25-year-old—half his age—would be envious of.

A 'prenup' had been in place and signed by Joanna, his then puzzled fiancé. Why should he need one? She only loved him and could not have cared less if they lived in a cardboard box.

Jeremy had tried to convince her it was for her own security, really, just in case anything should happen to him. Joanna wasn't stupid, though. She was aware it would prevent her from taking a sizeable chunk of his wealth and company should anything go wrong between them and divorce proceedings were to take place.

No, he definitely hadn't gone on holiday with Lena. And his wife, Joanna, was nowhere to be seen. His brain raced, trying to figure out the possibilities. If he had been going to a conference or meeting, he would have used the company jet, so why was he on a ship? It was a very nice ship, however, but despite that fact, why was he there?

As he tried to figure out why he was on board, a relaxed male voice from behind him interrupted his train of thought.

"Just enjoy the ride, dude."

Jeremy twisted around to see who had spoken to him. Next to him was what he considered a repugnant man, lying on a lounger. Jeremy thought it strange that he had only noticed this man when he spoke, as he had only moments ago looked around, trying to get his bearings.

This man had his hands clasped together and resting on his rotund stomach, which was clad in a dirty T-shirt emblazoned with the name 'Ramones' above a white logo. The T-shirt was having to work hard, as it barely contained the huge, sickeningly hairy stomach beneath.

The elastic band of his grey jogging bottoms had disappeared under the fold of fat that was the man's midriff. The hair on his head that had not seen the contents of a shampoo bottle in some time, let alone the inside of a barber's shop. It draped from the man's head with errant strands of his greasy hair catching on his stubbled jaw, which had been clearly there for at least a week.

The aroma emanating from this creature was as nauseating to Jeremy's nose as the sight was an assault on his eyes. Jeremy looked forward and muttered the words 'what the f—' when the man spoke again.

"Honestly dude, chill. I've never been on anything like this before in my entire life, but I'm sure what you're supposed to do is relax. Which works for me just fine," the slob said.

Jeremy turned around on his lounger and faced the man. As vile as he may be, this poor excuse of a human may be aware how he got there and, more to the point, how the hell both of them were on the same ship? No way could this slob afford a trip like this. He knew that diplomacy was the only way forward if any information was to be gleaned.

"Relax. OK, I can do that. So, how long you been on this cruise? I'm Jeremy, by the way."

"Marcus. Pleased to meet you, Jez," he replied.

Marcus kept his eyes closed as he greeted his new friend with a 'thumbs up' from his fat, grubby left hand and placed it back on his stomach.

Jeremy remembered when he used to represent people similar to this back in the days when he was a young lawyer, cutting his teeth on the legal system. However, since his meteoric rise through hard work, his clients had more zeros on their bank balance than he had inches around his waist. It was way below him to deal with plebs like this. There was nothing these people could offer him. That was, until now.

Jeremy feigned a smile and continued his conversation.

"So—Marcus. This may sound stupid, but do you remember me boarding this ship?"

"Yep—" Marcus started nonchalantly.

"You remember?" Jeremy interrupted.

"Nope. I was going to say, yes, it *does* sound stupid. You don't remember coming on board? You been smoking some good shit?" Marcus continued.

Marcus opened his eyes and glanced over at Jeremy, hoping that his new friend may donate some of whatever he had been smoking.

"Man! Check you out in the Armani!"

Jeremy suddenly halted and looked down at his torso. He was still wearing his tailor made grey suit and white shirt, one of many he had made for the office. The laces in his black Christian Louboutin shoes would have cost more than this man's entire wardrobe.

"Yes, yes. Whatever. As daft as it sounds, though, do you recall how we got here?" Jeremy persisted.

Marcus sat up, perching his heavy body on the edge of the lounger. With his forearms resting on his widespread knees and leaning forward, he thought for a moment, then shook his head.

"I don't know how *you* got here, man. I must have won a competition or something, as all I remember is I was on the stairway of my apartment. Can't remember what was happening. The next thing is I'm here. I have some pretty strong weed back in my pad. It's not the first time I've lost track of time—days even."

Marcus rose, propping his upper body on his knees with his hands.

"Tell you what. How about if I come with you to find out how you got on here? Someone must've come on board with you. Anyways, I could do with a bite to eat, so let's go."

Because of his immense size, he rose, struggling to stand, pulling his T-shirt over his stomach, and smiled at Jeremy.

"Come on dude, let's go find your mommy and daddy...Only joking dude."

Marcus gave a little snort and shuffled from the side of his lounger.

Jeremy looked at his watch, cursing under his breath that he had to oblige this slob purely because he did not know what was happening. And why he was on this ship?

"God dammit."

"What's up, bro?" Marcus turned to see what the frustration was all about.

"My watch has stopped. Unless it's twenty past eight in the evening."

Marcus looked down at his own watch that was digging into his chubby wrist and sniggered, looking back at Jeremy.

"Don't sweat it, dude. Mine's stopped too."

"But yours isn't a Patek Phillipe." Jeremy complained.

Marcus looked at his own watch.

"I don't go into that Asian stuff. Mine's a cheapo from the local store. My mom bought me it. She even put new batteries in it only last week and it's not working too. It says it's straight eight o'clock. Strange."

Jeremy shook his head in disbelief.

"Asian stuff?"

"Yeah, that Patek stuff. Not for me. I'm happy with this Casio. Good old American shit."

Marcus cleared the sun loungers and walked past Jeremy.

"Patek Phillipe is Swiss made. Jesus! Don't you know anything? Plus, I think you'll find that good old *American shit* on your wrist is Japanese." Jeremy said to the rancid, sweaty vapour trail as Marcus passed.

The young man paused, thought for a moment, then replied.

"I may not know watches, dude, but I ain't the one asking about how I got on a ship and where it's going to. You coming or what?"

Marcus waddled along the decking, bumping into any loungers that lay in his way.

"If it's Swiss, then is it expensive?" Marcus called back.

"Only about a hundred and twenty thousand." Jeremy replied.

"Dollars?"

Marcus stopped, swiftly turned around, and looked at the smartly dressed man.

A single look clearly conveyed Jeremy's frustration.

"Yes...dollars."

"I can understand why you're pissed if it cost you that much and it ain't working... Japanese, eh? Who'd a guessed, right?"

Jeremy looked at his watch again to make sure it had stopped, cursed, and then followed Marcus.

Chapter 2

The evening was silent, with only the faint sound of the waves licking the side of the ship, breaking the stillness. Jeremy, who had caught up to Marcus, looked out over the inky black sea.

The full moon was rising, with its pattern of craters shining down on the sea and ship. A puzzled look crept over Jeremy's face as he stared at the moon. Something wasn't quite right, but he just couldn't work out what.

To be a highly successful and obscenely paid lawyer meant you had to have a keen eye for detail, and Jeremy Leadstone's eyes were sharper than any adversary.

There wasn't a prosecution lawyer who could match his skills and ability. He twisted the truth to such a degree that even when faced with compelling video evidence, DNA, and eyewitnesses, Mr Leadstone's clients could still walk free. Yet, he could not put his finger on what the issue was with the rising moon.

"Beautiful, isn't it?" Marcus said, as he noticed his friend looking out to sea.

"Sorry?"

Jeremy's thoughts came back to the present.

"La Luna," Marcus tried to sound intellectual and mysterious.

Distracted for a brief second, Jeremy continued to gaze at the moon.

"Yes. Yes, it is."

"Quarter of a million miles away, you know," Marcus said, raising his eyebrows. "I got that off a science programme I was watching the other day."

"Fascinating," Jeremy said with an air of sarcasm. "Is it me, or is there something wrong with the moon?"

Marcus burst out with a brief laugh.

"Dude. If it's not where you are and how you got there, here...you know what I mean, it's thinking there's something wrong with the moon."

He gave a slight, but friendly, reassuring pat on Jeremy's shoulder.

"Honestly dude. You need to give me your weed dealer's number."

"Seriously, though. I mean. Something just isn't right. Look at the moon. There's something wrong. I just can't figure what. And it's quiet. Too damn quiet. No seagulls hitching a lift, nothing. Look!" Jeremy pointed up towards the sky. "It's a clear sky, yet there're no stars."

Marcus shrugged off the observations.

"I live in New York. You can have a clear sky in the dead of night and still have no stars. Light pollution, dude."

"But this isn't New York, is it?" Jeremy replied.

"Well, I'd hope not. Otherwise, the guys in the apartments below me are in trouble. It's that or I'm tripping my ass off."

"And something else. Where is everyone?" Jeremy continued.

He then paused and looked around at the empty deck.

"They just probably inside having some food. I hear these buffits are all you can eat." Marcus' eyes lit up with his own mention of food.

"Christ. Its buffet. It has a silent *T*. Buffet."

"Silent like the ship, hey?"

Marcus smiled at Jeremy and slowly wandered on.

"Aren't you the slightest bit bothered? I mean, you're on a ship. Christ knows how you got on. You sure as hell couldn't afford to pay to be on one—"

"Hey man. Too harsh! You don't know me," he said, cutting into Jeremy's insult.

Marcus stood upright and confronted his abuser.

"You don't know me at all. For all you know, I could be one of those crazy millionaires. Y'know, who dresses like this."

"And don't know what a Patek Phillipe is. Yeah, I can accept you being one of those millionaire crazies." Jeremy fired back, loaded with sarcasm.

Marcus decided not to bother arguing, as it seemed like too much hassle.

"OK. I'm not a millionaire, but I'm helping you out bro and you dis me like that? What's got your panties riding so far up your ass?"

"I am on a ship and I don't know how I got here. There's something strange about this whole thing and now I've gone and hurt some guy's feelings who I really couldn't give a shit about." Jeremy retorted.

"Screw you, man. I didn't have to help you. All I wanted to do was lie back and enjoy the ride but, no, I decided to help you and this is the thanks I get. Well, screw you." Marcus puffed up his chest and straightened his T-shirt. "Find your own damn way around here. I'm going to get some food and go back and lay down on my sun bed thing and chill."

Marcus tried pushing past Jeremy on his quest for free food, when a gentle hand placed on his chest stopped him.

"I'm sorry if I offended you, but I'm so confused right now and don't know if this is just a bad dream or what." Jeremy said with his expertly delivered—false—apology.

Marcus paused and looked at the man next to him.

"Dude, you were so far outta line, but I understand why."

Jeremy knew he had come back from another sticky situation, but before he could continue his lie, another voice broke the air.

"Hello? Mr Leadstone, Mr Hall?"

The two looked back and saw Manny smiling, standing next to their sun loungers.

"I have a bourbon with ice for you, sir, and for you, Mr Hall, I have a large packet of cheesy puffs and a bottle of Coke. That is what you wanted, wasn't it, sir?"

A smile came across Marcus' face as he shuffled and jogged back to the waiting crew member.

Jeremy, in frustration, looked down and dragged his hand through his hair, combing it back.

"Jesus...right, thank you Manny. I'm coming."

Jeremy looked again at the moon and studied it. He was trying to figure out what was wrong, but still the answer did not present itself.

"I'll just put it down here for you, sir." Manny called out as he placed the tumbler on a small table next to the sun lounger.

"Thanks...yes, I'm coming."

The voice in the back of Jeremy's head was screaming at him, telling him that something was seriously wrong. Whilst it had something to do with the moon, the puzzled lawyer could not figure it out.

Chapter 3

Marcus had already resumed his position, opened the packet of cheesy puffs and was munching eagerly on the orange curls as Jeremy reached the sun lounger. Jeremy bent down and picked up his glass, downing the golden brown liquid in one, leaving the ice cubes to dance in the tumbler as he slammed the glass on the table. Turning to the server as he was walking away, Jeremy called him back.

"Manny? Could you help me?"

"Yes, of course, sir. What can I do? Another bourbon?"

"Well, that as well, but where am I?"

Manny smiled and stood upright, puffing his chest out with pride.

"You are on the Pendentes. A beautiful yacht measuring one hundred and twenty-five metres. It measures nineteen metres at the beam and has a weight of seven thousand nine hundred tons. It has a top speed of fifty knots, not the fastest I grant you, but they built her for comfort, not speed—"

"Bit like myself," Marcus interrupted with a smile.

"It has a maximum capacity of one hundred souls, but right now there are only a few dozen." Manny smiled. "Which means I can do my job and attend to you and every request you may have."

"OK, thank you for the detailed breakdown of the ship, but where are we?" Jeremy said with an air of frustration.

"We are sailing South and will be at your destination within a couple of hours, sir."

"And where the hell is that? Manny!"

Manny bowed his head and with a smile, replied.

"Oh, I'm sorry sir, but I do so many journeys I do sometimes forget which one I'm on. I'm sure you'll remember when we get there, sir."

"I'm a God damn lawyer and I know when I'm being lied to, Manny."

"And a very good one you were, sir. How about if I get the captain to come and have a word with you, sir? He may give you more information. Would that be alright, sir?"

Before Jeremy could reply, Manny gave a quick nod of his head and made his way swiftly away from the escalating situation.

Jeremy placed his hands on his hips and tried to figure out his next move.

"Shit," he said through gritted teeth.

"Dude, just chill. It's a beautiful evening, the moon's rising, the sea is calm, and the sky is clear. Just sit down and relax."

"Is that all you do? Just relax? Aren't you motivated to do anything? You don't even care how you got here! Aren't you the slightest bit concerned?"

"With guys like you running around, I figure there's enough fuss already, without me joining in. So, yes, I relax. It's easy. You should try it sometime. It's good for your soul. Honestly, dude, you're going to have a heart attack."

Jeremy suddenly felt a sharp pain in his chest and a niggling sensation in the back of his mind tried to make him remember something. A loud cracking noise, like a gunshot or a balloon popping, sounded in his head. Jeremy rubbed his chest where the pain was, as Marcus continued.

"See, dude...? heart attack."

"No. It's just a little heartburn. I'm fine," Jeremy felt he had to defend himself.

"Well, if that's heartburn, you've some serious acid causing that!"

As he looked down at Marcus, Jeremy noticed his gaze fixed on something or someone towards the back of the ship and turned to see what he was looking at. Casually walking towards them was a young woman.

"I see what you mean," he whispered as Marcus stared with a handful of cheesy puffs.

Chapter 4

The young woman hadn't noticed the two men, one of which was staring at her as she focussed her gaze on the decking two feet in front of her. Her long wavy blonde hair marginally covered her face, but allowed the onlookers to gaze over her perfectly sculptured nose and lips.

Her expertly shaped eyebrows hovered above two blacker than black eyelashes that covered her almond-shaped blue eyes. Jeremy could see that an excellent plastic surgeon had worked on her body as her breasts were just the right size and shape under her designer tight white T-shirt.

He could see that she had spent many hours in a gym to achieve a body like that. It was also accepted that maybe a little help from a surgeon's knife might have played a part in sculpting her body. Her slender right arm was bent at the elbow where her manicured fingers softly held diamante encrusted cell phone.

"Hello, miss?" Jeremy broke the awkward silence.

The young lady suddenly stopped and looked up with a jump of surprise.

"Oh God. I'm sorry I didn't see you there," the young lady said, smiling and showing a perfect set of brilliant white teeth.

"It's OK. I figured as much so thought I'd let you know we were here before you walked into us...to avoid a collision?" Jeremy said.

"I'm Marcus," Marcus said, not wanting to be left out of the conversation.

Marcus sat up on the lounger, wiping his orange stained fingers on his jogging pants.

"Yeah. What he said. I'm Jeremy. Jeremy Leadstone. Attorney at law...and you are?"

Jeremy always felt that adding his job title left the other person in awe. Especially women like the one in front of him. He would never hold his hand out to greet them as he felt that, whilst enjoying impressing them, they were considerably below him and didn't deserve his hand.

"Hi Jeremy, I'm Christine."

Marcus just waved a resigned hand, as he noticed she had completely ignored his own introduction and laid back down and continued with his cheesy puffs.

"Please don't take it as a come on, but can I ask you a question?" Jeremy said, inadvertently giving Christine's breasts a cursory glance.

Christine's smile broadened, noticing the glance, and pushed her chest out even more.

"Sure," she said through brilliant white teeth.

"Do you remember coming on board this ship?"

Disappointed that the question was not regarding her or her very expensive body, Christine released her smile. She thought about the question, and whilst realising it was not about her, it was a good question. And one that she did not have an answer to.

Jeremy noticed the baffled look on the young woman's face that quickly disappeared. Not wanting to sound like the stereotypical 'dumb blonde' and say she didn't know, Christine lied.

"Yes, of course! What a silly question. Don't you?" Christine said, furrowing her brow, attempting to mock the attractive man in front of her.

"Actually, no. No, I don't," Jeremy replied.

Christine recognised the conversation wasn't going well, so changed the topic.

"What do you think of my ass?"

Christine turned to show the two men her tight fitted jeans and enhanced buttocks.

"Oh, jeez! Nice. Very nice," Marcus said, nearly choking on a mouth of cheesy puffs.

Jeremy kept his cool as he had come across women like this before. Lena was one of them.

"Yes. Very nice. Now, do you recall where we boarded?" Jeremy said, dismissing the request to compliment the young woman.

Not giving up on an elusive compliment, Christine moved slightly, so the smartly dressed man could see more of the seat of her jeans and continued with her quest for appreciation.

"I had it done recently, in Mexico. The surgeon was amazing! It only cost me five hundred dollars." Christine continued, turning to face her audience.

"I had my boobs fixed in Miami. I had a tummy tuck, lips, and nose in London. Harley Street is very expensive, but don't you think they were worth it?"

She twisted slightly from side to side and smiled, allowing her audience to experience her perfection in full.

"Yeah. Stunning. Not a penny wasted. Now, where did we board?" Jeremy said, who accepted that her body was pleasant to look at, but had seen much better on some of his female clients.

Christine sensed the sarcasm in the compliment, but accepted it, anyway.

"Oh, it was in that port. Oh, what's it called now?"

Christine was a poor liar; she always had her body to help her with any deception. However, when she faced someone who was unresponsive to her curves and beauty, that threw her.

"Yeah, I thought so. You don't know either," Jeremy said with a raised eyebrow, indicating he had sussed her out.

"Oh, I don't know! I jet off to so many places. I can't expect to remember every place I visit."

Christine felt the best form of defence was attack.

"And how many times do you *jet off* on a ship?" Jeremy enquired.

She was rapidly losing this battle so went on the defensive, in her usual way. With a flick of her hair and a bat of her eyelashes, she slipped into her 'cute' mode. Jeremy had seen this tactic so many times in court that he had his own look that let the woman know it would not work. Christine received the look and knew right away what it meant.

"OK, so I don't remember. So what? What you going to do? Sue me? You said you don't remember either. So you're no better than me," she said with a hint of bitterness, knowing she had lost.

"I never said I was better than you. I never thought that for one second. I just want to know how I got on here and where the hell this ship is going?" Jeremy said.

He knew himself that his mental superiority and wealth contradicted this equality statement.

"Maybe I can help with that, sir."

Manny appeared seemingly from nowhere with a tray in his hand.

"I have spoken to the captain and whilst I'm afraid he is busy right now, as soon as he is finishes what he is doing, he will come see you, sir. Oh, and Miss Sommers? Here's your Svalbardi bottled water, with a twist of lime as you requested."

Jeremy turned to the waiter.

"And how will he know how to find me?" Jeremy's tone was one of frustration.

"It's not a big ship, Mr Leadstone, plus Captain Obol is very good at finding his passengers. He knows everyone who boards this ship, as he personally accepted each one of you on board."

"Obol? What sort of name is that?" Christine said mockingly.

"It is Greek, miss. Your captain is Captain Charon Obol. He is the best I have ever served under. He does his job supremely well and you can guarantee he will get you to your destination on time and in the comfort you are accustomed to," Manny said.

The waiter gave a courteous nod of the head and left the group.

"Svalbardi? How much have you just paid for that?" Jeremy asked, knowing exactly what the price tag was for a bottle of water that had come directly from an iceberg.

Christine felt she was being scolded, like her father used to do, and resented Jeremey's tone.

"It's the best, and it's my money and I'll spend it how I want, thank you very much. Anyway, as far as I'm aware, there's no charge. It's all free."

She felt for the first time she had the upper hand, knowing that the drinks were free.

Marcus' ears pricked up and looked at his packet of cheesy puffs and coke.

"Still. It's just water," Jeremy said dismissively. "Anyway. I'm off to find this Captain Obol and find out exactly where we started and where the hell we're going to. Are you coming?"

Jeremy glanced at both Christine and Marcus.

Christine looked down at Marcus and curled her top lip in disgust.

"Yes, I'll come," she said.

"I'll stay here if it's all the same," Marcus said, as he placed his snacks on his stomach and leant over to take a drink.

Christine looked up at Jeremy and smiled.

"Shall we go?" she said.

"Sure you're going to be alright on your own here?" Jeremy said to Marcus, who was taking a deep drink of cola.

Marcus casually waved them off, wiping his mouth with the back of his other hand.

"I'll be fine. Off you go. You know where to find me if you want me."

Christine looked at Jeremy with raised eyebrows as if to say, 'not that we'd ever need or want him'.

Chapter 5

Jeremy placed his hand on Christine's lower back, escorting her away from the belching slob, taking the lead, and headed towards the rear of the ship.

When she considered it was safe to speak without Marcus hearing, Christine commented on her disgust about how someone could let themselves go so much. Jeremy had to agree.

To do nothing and not want anything but to live a life like that was beyond him. 'More' was definitely better, according to Jeremy. 'More' knowledge meant more power, which meant more money. 'More' was so much better.

The couple slowly walked in silence to the back of the ship. Jeremy looking in every direction, trying his best to find something that made sense or gave a clue where they were, whilst Christine looked down at her cleavage and admired how it moved as she walked.

"Are you OK? You always seem to look downwards." Jeremy enquired.

Christine, looking up and smiling, replied.

"I'm fine. I spent a lot of money on these boobs, and I just love the way they move. Don't you agree?"

"Oh, really. Yes, they're very nice."

Jeremy was not interested in the cleavage of the young woman. He'd seen much better on his wife, Joanna, and had probably spent more on them than this young bimbo had. Christine just seemed to be one of those 'Stepford' women who felt they had to look beautiful. They had to have everything perfect and in a certain way. Jeremy knew that perfection was not about everything being perfect, it was about looking natural, and Christine's body, whilst nice, was not natural.

As they reached the rear of the ship, Jeremy leaned on the stern's balustrade and looked out. The air was warm; it was a clear evening, not a star in the sky. To his left, the moon was rising higher in the darkening sky. The voice in his head was still saying that something was wrong and whatever it was, was still eluding him.

In a flash, Jeremy felt a presence and turned to see what or who it was. A man in his early thirties was running towards the couple with a look of abject fear in his eyes. Quickly shielding Christine, Jeremy prepared for an attack. The young man ran to the balustrade close to the couple, climbed over the railings, and looked at the startled Christine.

"I've seen him! I've seen him! The captain! I've seen the real him!" the man shouted. "I know!"

Jeremy looked at the man in wonder, stunned by his statement.

"Know what? Do you know where we are or where we're going?" he shouted back. "Wait. You don't need to do this. Come back and we can sort this out, I'm sure. Hey, what's your name? Come on now, can you just come away from the edge and we can talk about this? What do you mean, you've seen the actual captain?"

The man looked at Jeremy with dreaded fear in his eyes that Jeremy had only seen once before. In his early years, he had lost his one and only case that had ended up with his client sitting in the electric chair.

"Are you talking about Charon Obol? Who is he really?" Jeremy pleaded.

The man inhaled as if to tell Jeremy and Christine more about the captain when all three heard the padding of running feet. The man's eyes widened and looked over to see three cabin crew appearing from where he had come from.

"Sir...! Mr Cartwright. Come back! The waters are dangerous. Don't jump!"

Chapter 6

Jeremy and Christine quickly glanced at the cabin crew, who were attempting to stop the man from jumping, raising their hands to calm the situation down. The couple then looked back at him, but it was too late. The man had released his grip on the balustrade and jumped into the darkness.

Jeremy ran over to where the man had stood and looked to see where he had landed, but there was no sign of him. There wasn't even the sound of a splash.

"What the hell?" Jeremy looked dumbfounded. "Where'd he go?"

"Sir. Miss. Please come away from the edge. It's not safe."

Without looking at the crew members, Jeremy screamed at them to stop the ship and get help.

"Sir, I'm sorry it's too late. He's gone," one of the crew members said, who had approached Jeremy and had taken hold of his arm, gently pulling him away from the balustrade.

"What d'you mean it's too late? Get some help now! You have a passenger overboard. Surely it's your duty to try to rescue him!"

Jeremy broke free from the gentle grip and looked back over the balustrade. Questions formulated and race around his brain.

"Where did he go? There wasn't a splash. And what did he mean, he had seen the captain?" Jeremy asked to the other crew who had approached Christine and tried to shield her from the view.

"Sir, we have some passengers who are not well, sir. They think all sorts of things and it disturbs them. This is not the first time that something like this has happened, and I'm afraid these waters are less than forgiving. Please sir, if I may," the lead crew member said as he looked at Jeremy and smiled reassuringly.

He ushered the couple to the row of sun loungers at the stern of the ship and offered the seats to them.

"Can we get you anything? A drink perhaps? Bourbon with ice for the gentleman and for the lady. Another water?"

"Listen! I am Jeremy Leadstone. I am an attorney—"

"Yes sir, I am aware you were very good indeed," the lead member butted in.

"Don't interrupt me. What the hell is going on here? I am an attorney and I know when someone is lying to me and so far there's an increasing smell of bullshit around here. Why won't you help him for God's sake? Why didn't I hear a splash when that man jumped? When did this journey start and where the hell are we going?"

The crew member passively held his hands up.

"Sir, I can't explain why you didn't hear the splash. Maybe it was the noise of everything else, or maybe it was down to the sheer surprise of what had happened. Maybe it was that which blocked out the sound. I believe your waiter, Manny, has spoken to the captain, who has said he will come and see you and explain everything."

"Oh, screw this. We're going to find the captain ourselves," Jeremy said, boiling with frustration.

"We are?" Christine asked.

"Damn right we are. Something is seriously wrong here and I am going to find out, one way or another, what is going on."

Jeremy placed a firm hand on Christine's back and ushered her away from the crew members.

"Keep walking. We need to get away from these goons. Something isn't right here. This whole damned cruise isn't right," Jeremy whispered, quietly to the shocked Christine.

Chapter 7

Jeremy and Christine swiftly walked along the port side of the ship with Christine almost having to break into a jog.

"Can we slow down, please?" Christine said, who was becoming annoyed with her new acquaintance.

Christine stopped and stood her ground. Men had pushed her around all her life. That was until last year, when she took charge and made some drastic changes to her life and appearance.

Jeremy looked at her and recognised a glare of defiance in her eyes. He had always got what he wanted in the past, but here was a woman standing up to him, which was something he wasn't used to, out of court anyway. The circumstances in which he found himself in were also unusual and because of that, he decided to be less forceful.

"Sorry, but something was seriously wrong with everything back there."

"Oh, D'you think?" Christine said with a heavy air of sarcasm.

A sudden pain striking Jeremy's chest and a loud crack sounding in his head hit him full on, causing Jeremy to wince and grab his chest.

"Are you alright?" Christine asked when she saw how much pain he was in.

Jeremy shook his head to rid himself of the pain.

"Just a little heartburn. It's nothing," Jeremy lied, as he didn't know what had caused the pain or what the sound was.

"Look, I have been a lawyer for probably longer than you have been alive. I have seen and heard things in my life that enable me to know when something is wrong. I don't believe a word those crew members said. That was total bullshit."

Jeremy looked into Christine's eyes and continued.

"Does any of this seem right to you? We don't know how we got on this godforsaken ship, or where we're going. A man takes his own life, saying he's seen the captain. I mean, what the hell is that all about? Then the crew doesn't even try to rescue him, but calls him a whacko instead. Then when he jumps, there's no splash or floating body being left behind."

"I don't think they called him a whacko—"

"You know what I mean."

"I just don't think it's nice, that's all, calling someone a whacko."

"Jesus Christ!"

Frustrated, Jeremy looked up from his companion and noticed a glass-panelled door leading into what appeared to be a lounge bar.

"Tell you what. Let's go in here, have a drink and see if anyone else in there can help, or knows anything. There can't be just us two who find this whole thing bizarre," Jeremy said, trying to diffuse the situation.

"OK, but there's only one who finds this bizarre. One of us finds this quite upsetting. That poor man. What was he thinking? I'll admit it was strange not to hear a splash, though. I suppose a drink could help with the upset. How do I look?" Christine said briefly, shaking her hair and giving a little pout to Jeremy.

"You look great," Jeremy said, not really looking, his comment heavily laced with insincerity.

Chapter 8

The couple entered the ship's bar and met with a warm greeting from the bartender.

"Good evening, Mr Leadstone, Miss Sommers. Bourbon with ice for you, sir? And a Bombay gin with tonic and a twist of lemon for you, miss?"

The bartender was just polishing a glass when he greeted them. He gently placed the towel under the bar, along with the sparkling tumbler. Two crystal vases flanked the bar displaying stunning white lilies.

"Yes, please," Christine said with a smile.

"I love the smell of lilies, don't you?" Christine whispered to Jeremy.

The young woman scanned the room to see if anyone had noticed her and her figure. Christine then led Jeremy to a pair of empty bar stools at the bar, close to the bartender, who was now pouring a large bourbon over two bricks of ice.

As Jeremy sat down, Christine perched herself on a stool next to him, expertly arching her back so anyone behind her could experience the full glory of her tight fitted jeans. With more of a query than concern, Christine looked towards Jeremy.

"You don't look like a person who would suffer heartburn. Are you sure you're alright?" she asked.

Jeremy had seldom had heartburn before. He had kept himself in the best possible shape, as he needed to be mentally and physically strong enough to run his law firm. He needed to be sharp for any taking over, or destroying, of the competition as and when it was required. Was it this ship that had given him the heartburn? What was that cracking bang in his head? Was the sound from a distant memory that had resurfaced, triggered by his current situation?

Jeremy shut out the chest pain and focussed on the matter at hand.

"I'm fine. Absolutely nothing to worry about," he said with a smile.

The bartender interrupted the pregnant pause between the couple by placing two drinks in front of them, along with two napkins with small logos of lily flowers in the corner. Both thanking the bartender, Christine with a smile and Jeremy with a nod of his head, they each took a sip and eased into their seats. Christine who broke the brief silence.

"I understand that you're concerned about this ship, but for me, it just seems... natural, apart from that poor guy. That was strange, and you're right, why didn't they help him? It may sound silly, but being on the ship and all that, I just don't think it is as important to me as it is to you. Don't ask me why, I don't know."

Christine took another sip from her glass.

Jeremy looked at the young woman, initially in disbelief.

'How could anybody not be concerned? I mean, being in a place and you are not sure how you got here? Typical dumb bitch, all that matters to this one is trying to have admirers lusting after her looks. Jesus,' he thought, and raised his tumbler.

Before taking a drink, a mature female voice behind him broke his focus.

"Thank you so much, Manny. Oh, could I have some salt, please?"

Jeremy turned to see who had spoken and noticed a morbidly obese woman in her mid-60s, sat at a table close to the rear of the lounge. In front of her was a mountain of fries on a platter, flanked by chocolate cake and a full champagne flute. The waiter swiftly walked to a small table at the other side of the bar and retrieved a salt cellar, bringing it back to the woman, like a dog with a ball to its owner.

"There you are, madam. If there's anything else you require, just call me," the waiter said with a smile.

"Thanks again Manny. You're a doll," the woman said, with a fork full of fries ready to be devoured.

Jeremy, taking a sip of his bourbon, put the tumbler on the bar.

"I'll be back shortly. I'm just going to talk to this woman," he said to Christine with his gaze firmly fixed on the old woman. "See if she knows anything."

Christine looked in the same direction as Jeremy.

"Oh my God! How do you let yourself get that big?" Christine whispered, and looked away in disgust.

Jeremy felt a certain amount of revulsion for the woman himself as he walked over to her. She was obviously wealthy, as seen by her skin tone, which was clearly pampered with every conceivable face cream going.

Her beautifully coiffured hair was the sort that only let a seven-hundred-dollar stylist anywhere near it, and her dress at one time would have been very expensive, but through time had lost its lustre.

"Excuse me. May I?" Jeremy said to the woman, looking towards a chair at the other side of her table.

"Sure thing, honey. Would you like a bite to eat? I can get Manny to bring you something," the woman said, smiling at the young man in front of her.

Jeremy refused the kind offer by holding up one hand and a smile, then pulled out a chair from the table.

"Thank you, but no. I wonder if I could ask you a question," he said, sitting down.

"Honey, I'm way too old for you. Anyway, I don't think your girlfriend would like it. Do you?" she said with a knowing smile, eyeing up Christine at the bar.

Quickly registering the weak joke, Jeremy played along. Giving a chuckle, he replied.

"Oh, I don't know. She's quite open-minded...no, could I ask you about your waiter?" Jeremy said, keeping his voice low so as not to be heard by 'the ever ready,' waiter.

"Manny? Sure anything. He's a really nice guy. What would you like to know?"

Jeremy leaned closer.

"Is Manny his real name?"

Realising he had not introduced himself, he added.

"I'm sorry. My name is Jeremy."

The woman smiled, wiping her mouth with a nearby napkin.

"Marianne. Marianne Connor. Please to meet you doll. No, Manny isn't his real name. He said that his real name was 'too complicated' to pronounce, so I was just to call him Manny. Nice ass on him, though." Marianne smiled with a glint in her eye.

"I hadn't noticed," Jeremy said, returning the smile.

"I'm not surprised, having that by your side. She's a cutie. You know, my tits were that firm years ago. But not plastic, like hers," Marianne added with an air of scorn.

Jeremy tried not to picture the image and continued with his questioning.

"Just one more question, if I may...do you remember getting on this ship?"

"Honey. My husband was a multi-millionaire with his own company, before he died, bless him. Now I'm constantly on cruise ships. They're all the same to me. They just blend into one. Do I remember getting on this one? No, I don't. I don't even know where we're going, but I'm sure it'll be somewhere warm. It always is. I love the sun, don't you? As is always the case, the food is free and keeps coming, so I'm happy," Marianne said, looking adoringly at the platter in front of her.

"Hello Mr Leadstone, sir. Would you like me to bring your drink over?"

Manny appeared at the table with a courteous bow and smile.

"Manny, isn't it?" Jeremy said, looking at the waiter.

"It is, sir."

"Funny. I had a waiter serving me a drink on the other side of the ship and he was called Manny, too. Looked nothing like you," Jeremy said with a tone difficult to mistake as anything else but what it was. The beginning of an interrogation.

Manny continued to smile at his customer.

"Can I ask how many Mannys' are there on board?" Jeremy asked.

"Oh, I couldn't say sir."

Jeremy looked at the waiter with an intense stare. Being a lawyer, he recognised a lie when he heard one.

"Couldn't or wouldn't, Manny?"

"I don't know what you mean, sir," the waiter maintained his smile. "Anyway, if you need anything, just give me a wave and I'll be right over, Mr Leadstone."

"Something tells me you know exactly what I mean, *Manny*. So what is it? Couldn't or wouldn't? You know what, let me guess. You don't know, but you're sure the captain will fill me in when I see him."

Jeremy stared deep into the waiter's eyes. This usually made the recipient of this stare very uncomfortable, but for some reason, it didn't seem to work.

In fact, the opposite was happening. Jeremy looked into Manny's eyes and saw a deep, disturbing blackness. Whilst his waiter wore a pleasant and helpful smile, his eyes were conveying another message. It was as if someone had sucked the life right out of his eyes, leaving a void of black, only visible to a close observer.

"I wasn't aware you were to see Captain Obol, but as you are, sir, then you'd be correct. I'm certain Captain Obol will answer all the questions you may have," the unflinching waiter said.

Chapter 9

As Jeremy strolled over to speak to the elderly woman, he left Christine sitting at the bar to wonder what on earth was happening. She cradled the stem of her gin glass as she faced the mirrored shelving that held a myriad of bottled sprits.

"Hello gorgeous. Can I buy you a drink?" came a voice from Christine's side.

Christine turned her head to see who had spoken to her and saw a man making himself comfortable on the barstool next to her.

"I'm fine, thank you. I already have one," she said, glancing at the drink in front of her, then at the man.

Christine briefly turned away, then returned, staring at the man.

"Tell me. Does that line ever work?" she asked disdainfully.

The man rested his elbows on the bar and smiled, showing his yellow stained teeth.

"That depends. It's opened up communication." He continued, turning to Christine "My name is James. James Duke."

Christine stifled a laugh as she pictured this man in his late 50s trying to do his best James Bond line. 'My name is Duke. James Duke.'

"And you are?" James added.

"Tired of men twice my age trying to hit on me. So if you please, leave me alone and try that line on someone else," Christine said with eyes that conveyed a much stronger sentiment.

James was a seasoned 'player' and had been on the receiving end of firmer brush-offs than this. The thought of seeing what was under that tight top was all he needed to continue his pursuit.

James knew that rolling up his sleeve to reveal what looked like an expensive watch on his hairy wrist was always a sure-fire way of getting the ladies to take an interest. James, brushing back his receding hair, continued.

"Oh, come on," he said playfully. "I'm only trying to be sociable. Anyway, I don't see you with anyone."

"Actually, she is with someone. Me."

Jeremy had come back and had seen Christine being bothered by this lecherous scumbag.

"Well, I'm up for a threesome, if that's your taste." James smiled, looking at his competition and then back at what he considered his prey.

Christine no longer suffered men like this who thought they were God's gift to women. She glared at him, turning to face James squarely on.

"Why don't you do what your hairline has done and disappear... just piss off," she said with a finger prodding his soft hairy chest.

Jeremy held back a smile. 'This girl has balls,' he thought. 'I'm beginning to like her.'

James was a stocky fifty-seven-year-old man, and whilst he accepted he could do with losing a few pounds, he was adamant he was a serious notch on any woman's bedpost.

His weakness was the one thing she had just attacked, and she did so with the force of a nuclear missile strike. James sat up, regaining some composure, and brushed his hair back again and feigned a laugh.

"Jeez lady. You're a feisty one," he said through a forced smile.

Jeremy joined in.

"And if you're trying to impress women with your fake Rolex Seamaster, then at least make it a decent fake."

"What d'you mean? It is a real Seamaster!" James protested, subtly rolling down his sleeve.

"No, it's not, because if it was a real Seamaster, then you'd know Rolex don't do Seamasters. Omega does. So why don't you go away now, and bother someone else," Jeremy fired back with his unrecoverable retort.

Fully covering up his watch with his right hand, James knew they had found him out and climbed down from the stool.

"The slut is all yours, buddy. Good luck. You'll need it with this plastic bitch."

As the last word left James' mouth, Christine's right hand met his genitals in a vice-like grip, buckling the man's knees.

"I strongly suggest you go away now before I rip your tiny balls off and hide them in a bowl of similar sized peanuts." Christine growled through gritted teeth.

The agonising look on James' face was that of a man who would do as requested, without question.

Christine glared at the man, releasing her grip on his crotch.

"Go on. Off you trot. Back to the hovel you came from." Christine said as she gave a patronising wave.

James shuffled away from the couple to a table further from the bar, cradling his tender testicles.

"So what was all that about, leaving me here to fend for myself? Some gent you are," Christine said as she turned to Jeremy with a withering look.

"It seems to me you can look after yourself with what I've just witnessed. Anyway, I just heard that woman over there say something which got my attention," he replied.

Christine raised her eyebrows and looked at Jeremy as if to say 'continue'.

"She called her waiter Manny. I went over and asked her about it and she said that he had asked to call him that as—"

"His name was too complicated to pronounce," Christine finished his sentence.

Christine raised her hand and turning to the bar, beckoned the bartender.

"Yes, Miss Sommers. Another 'G and T'?" the bartender said as he hopped over.

"Yes please, and a bourbon for my friend too, please," came the smiling request.

"Right away, miss."

The bartender smiled and was just about to turn away when Christine stopped him.

"Excuse me. Could I just ask you your name?"

"Just call me Manny. Everyone does. My name is a little hard to pronounce," he said.

The bartender turned and went for two clean glasses.

Christine looked back at Jeremy.

"Manny?" Christine mouthed the name. "What the hell?"

Moments later, Manny returned.

"There you go Miss Sommers, Mr Leadstone. Enjoy."

He placed the drinks, along with two paper napkins, on the bar.

Christine picked up both drinks and slid off her barstool.

"I think we need to sit down somewhere quiet," she said and wandered over to a spare table in a quiet part of the lounge.

Jeremy followed her, picking up the napkins as he left the bar.

Chapter 10

As the couple sat down, they huddled close to keep their conversation private. Christine began.

"OK, so now I'm a little worried. I understand what you said about being here, and yet I still feel like I should be. But all the crew being called Manny? OK, I'm a little spooked over that," she whispered.

"I know. Unless, of course, HR for the company had decided to only employ staff with long complicated names that no one could pronounce and make everyone answer to the name of Manny. Something stinks here," Jeremy replied.

"I get what you say about the stars. There should be tonnes in a clear sky. And why didn't those crew members raise the alarm for that guy? Isn't that illegal or something?" Christine said and took a sip from her glass.

Jeremy felt the pain in his chest and in the back of his mind, heard the loud bang again. Wincing and grabbing his chest, Jeremy let out a little groan.

"It's that pain in your chest again, isn't it? You sure you're not having a heart attack? My friend's uncle had a heart attack whilst on the tennis court. When the paramedics got there, it was too late. Do you need to see a doctor?" said Christine as she leaned closer to Jeremy.

Something was telling Jeremy what he was feeling wasn't a heart attack. Why was it he always thought he'd heard a loud bang a split second before the pain?

"I'm fine. Believe me," he said unconvincingly.

"Honestly?"

"I'm fine!" Jeremy said in a firmer tone.

Jeremy never used the word 'honest'. In his line of work and with the cases he had won, it just didn't seem right to use that word. He would always smile to himself. 'A lawyer with a conscience. Who'd a thought!' he would think to himself.

However, it still didn't take away this pain he was struggling with. It was a pain he'd never experienced before. What the hell was causing it? He was a healthy man and always kept himself fit. He needed to if he were to maintain his level of extra-marital activities.

'I'm surprised Joanna never found out. God, I must be good,' he thought.

"Anyway, back to what you were saying. I don't do maritime law, but whilst it would be wrong, I doubt they're breaking any laws by not sounding the alarm. But again, when the guy jumped in, why didn't we hear a splash? At that height, we should've heard something. OK, it was dark, but I didn't notice a body either. The sea simply doesn't swallow people. Even sharks who take their prey below the surface surely they'd make a noise. Nothing... It's like he just disappeared. And that just does not happen," Jeremy explained.

The couple stayed silent for a while, mulling over the facts.

Apart from the musak in the background and the low murmuring of the few other passengers, the lounge was quiet.

Jeremy looked into his tumbler and watched as he swirled the ice cubes around the base of his otherwise empty glass. Christine just stared out of a nearby window. She was thinking about what Jeremy had said about how they had boarded the ship, how she didn't remember, and more to the point, how come she didn't care?

She felt she was where she should be. But why? It made little sense. She raised and drained her gin glass, leaving the citrus slice perched on the ice.

Manny was about to walk over with his usual helpful smile when Jeremy stopped him with a 'Yes please,' and a nod of his head.

"Not for me, thanks. Could I have some water, please?" Christine added.

Halted in his tracks, Manny quickly nodded his head and returned to the bar. Moments later, he placed a whisky tumbler and a bottle of Svalbardi on the table.

The couple smiled at the waiter to convey their thanks and continued their secretive conversation.

"That's something else," Jeremy said. "Did you ever tell them what you liked to drink?"

"Well, yes. How else would they know?" Christine said.

"Exactly. How *would* they know? I never told them. Or at least I don't remember."

Christine looked at her unopened bottle in front of her and pondered over what she had just been told. Had she ever told them what she liked? She too couldn't remember ever telling 'the other Manny' her favourite tipple, whether on deck or in the bar. An idea exploded in Christine's head.

"Manny?" she called out. "I wonder if I could have a bite to eat, please?"

The waiter, who was standing near the bar, turned with a smile.

"Would you like your usual grilled chicken in wholemeal with low fat mayonnaise? Or would you like a cheeky little cheese burger with a slice of beef tomato?" Manny asked.

"You know what? I'm good, thanks. I'll leave it for now. Thanks anyway," Christine said, returning the smile.

Jeremy looked at her with a puzzled face. 'What was she up to?' Christine leant closer to her friend.

"I have ordered nothing on this ship, that's a fact. So how did he know my usual sandwich or my guilty secret?" she whispered.

Jeremy looked at her and was about to try the same thing when he stopped himself. What would be the point? He had already proven that fact.

"OK, now I'm a little worried," Christine said, looking at Jeremy to see if he had any comforting answers.

Jeremy's mind began frantically searching for a lead on where to go next.

'Give me a courtroom any day,' he thought.

Chapter 11

"OK. We need to locate this captain and find out why this guy did a swan dive just because he claimed he'd seen him. We also need to know what the hell is going on with this ship. And where the hell are we going? I still haven't figured out what's wrong with the bloody moon. I'm sure that has something to do with all this too," Jeremy said.

Jeremy scanned the lounge, scrutinising his fellow passengers.

Marianne was tucking into even more food, and that lecherous bastard Duke was hitting on another blonde female, who obviously had spent most of her time and money on her looks, rather than education.

There was one other noticeable person. Sat in the far corner was a man in his early forties; a bland, average looking male who could have easily been a private detective; he blended into obscurity so well. The only sign making him noticeable was the unwavering stare on his face. Jeremy was an expert at facial expressions. He could have been a wealthy man if he played poker, but he just loved the battle in a courtroom. To him it was like pieces on a chess board.

This man had a glare of pure hatred and had directed his loathing towards James Duke. He was watching the lecherous old bastard with a stare that screamed violence towards him. Jeremy puzzled over this for a moment and realised...he was jealous!

'This man was envious of the balding son of a bitch who was hitting on a blonde bimbo who was lapping up his patter. OK, this guy looked boring, but why on Earth would he be jealous over that guy, who was flashing a twenty-dollar fake Rolex at this woman?' Jeremy pondered.

The man had probably been there for some time by the looks of the three quarter empty bottle of whisky that was in front of him. By the side of the bottle was an empty tumbler keeping the bottle company on the table. Jeremy watched for a second, then his face dropped. Reading this man, Jeremy quickly picked up that something was about to happen. He was right.

The man sat upright, and with his gaze firmly fixed on the lecherous James Duke, he took a deep breath.

With his eyes still on Duke the man stood up, picking up the whisky bottle by its neck from the table and marched over to womaniser, who was commenting about his watch to the young female.

As the man reached the unsuspecting Duke, he raised the bottle above his head. Jeremy suddenly shouted out to stop, but it was too late. The bottle came crashing down on the back of Duke's head, sending shards of glass, whisky, and blood in all directions.

The young woman screamed in horror as the charming man who was showing her his expensive watch collapsed in front of her, drenching her in glass and whisky.

Christine heard the bone cracking collision between bottle and skull and turned to see where it came from and yelled.

"Oh, Christ!"

"You, son of a bitch! Bastards like you always get lucky. Well, not today," the attacker shouted as he stood over the unconscious and bleeding man. "I've had enough of you and your kind. You always get everything you want. It's not fair. When is it my turn?" he screamed at the barely conscious Duke.

Before Jeremy could get up to stop any further attack, three waiters pounced on the attacker and pinned him against a nearby wall.

"When do I get lucky? It's always your kind, isn't it? You bastard!" the man bellowed, trying to break free from the waiters.

Two more cabin crew burst into the lounge from outside and tended to the bleeding Duke, crumpled on the floor. Quickly covering the wound with a white towel, the two men picked him up, keeping him upright with an arm over each of their shoulders, and walked him out of the lounge. Aided by the crew, Duke staggered towards the door, dragging his feet as he went.

"It's OK sir, we'll take you to the medical room. You'll be fine, sir," one of his helpers said.

Jeremy and Christine watched as James Duke was helped to the door with the crew members flanking him.

"Oh, my God! I hope he's going to be alright," Christine said, not taking her eyes off James and the towel on his head that was becoming redder by the second.

Jeremy just watched as they took him out of the lounge.

"Jesus! Did you see that?" Christine said to Jeremy as the lounge door closed after the men had left.

"See that? Oh yes. But how the hell is that man alive? Let alone walking," Jeremy said.

"What d'you mean?"

"It's not like the movies when a guy gets hit on the back of the head by a bottle and continues on with the bar fight. I've seen photos in court of injuries sustained in attacks like this. The victim has been very lucky to stay alive. At the least, it would fracture the skull, so walking out of here, albeit with help, is still unbelievable."

Jeremy tore his gaze away from the exit and turned to Christine.

"Come on. We need to find out where they're taking him and how the hell is he not dead."

Jeremy quickly stood up and made his way to the door, with Christine following, leaving the struggling man and three crew members trying to calm him down.

As the lounge door opened and the couple exited, Jeremy watched James disappear down a flight of stairs helped by the staff, only yards further up the ship.

"Come on. This way," he said, and taking Christine by the wrist, rushed towards the stairway.

Chapter 12

The couple reached the stairway in a matter of seconds and looked down the stairs, expecting to see the struggling crew members and the badly injured man.

"What? Where are they?" Christine said. "I don't understand."

"Me neither," he whispered as he tried in vain to work it out.

Jeremy stared down the stairs at...nothing. No crew members, no injured man, no blood. Nothing. In a courtroom, Jeremy was well versed in explaining everything away. His client, with the weapon, with witnesses and on camera, was a walk in the park for a seasoned lawyer like him. But this? How was this even possible? It wasn't.

Moments passed by, the couple staring down the stairway and doing nothing else.

"Do you want to go down and look?" Christine asked, breaking the silence.

"Damn straight I do," Jeremy said, returning to his usual self.

The couple ventured down the wooden-topped metal steps into the blackness below. As they reached the bottom, both of them felt a chill. Something wasn't right. In fact, something was definitely wrong.

At the bottom of the steps of this luxuriously modern ship, there was a distinct change in atmosphere. From the mild, starless evening up on deck, which had an aroma of opulence and extravagance, to down below, which was very different.

Below was dark...pitch black. Not a single light on, not even a faint glow from any door jamb. The foreboding smell of old, damp, rotting wood had replaced the scent of polish and sumptuousness that had been dancing in the air on deck. Christine shivered.

"I don't think we're supposed to be down here," she said, whispering.

"Have you got your phone?" said Jeremy, turning in the darkness to Christine.

"Sure why?"

"Can I have it? Just turn the light on for me, please."

Christine tapped the phone's screen, and a cool torchlight immediately flooded the area. Taking the phone from his companion, Jeremy shone the light around.

"What the hell!"

"Oh, my god! I really don't like this. Can we leave?" Christine pleaded.

Wherever the phone's torch shone was not what they expected. How could a yacht looking so stunning on deck appear so old below? It looked like an old Spanish galleon with wooden planks for the hull. The planking looked like it had been submerged in water for hundreds of years.

"It's not possible," Jeremy said, stunned. "It's just not possible."

Below deck was one vast space with no rooms, no engine, no crew, or injured man.

"Where the hell did they go? What sort of ship is this?" Jeremy said, totally bewildered.

"I don't know," Christine said. "And I don't want to either. Can we go now?"

Aghast at what he was seeing; Jeremy quickly came to his senses.

"Sure. Let's get out of here."

As they swiftly turned to go back to the stairs, there, close behind them, and lit by the cell phone's torch, was a crew member.

"Can I help you, sir?"

Christine shrieked in surprise as the light illuminated the smiling crew member's face.

"I'm sorry if I startled you, miss. Can I help you?"

"Manny, is it?" Jeremy asked.

"Yes sir, it is. Can I be of help?"

Jeremy was struggling to process everything he had just seen, along with the shock of another crew member suddenly appearing from nowhere.

"What the hell is this?" Jeremy said after a brief second.

"What's what, sir?" Manny said, smiling.

"This!" Jeremy demanded.

Jeremy swung around with the torch and lit up a carpeted corridor full of cabin doors.

"I'm sorry, sir. The lights down here are usually on a motion sensor," smiled Manny, and waved his hand in the air.

With barely an audible click, all the lights in the corridor sparked to life, revealing a downstairs as plush as on deck.

"I'm sorry, sir, but sometimes the lights have a mind of their own. I'll get one of our crew to fix it."

"Where's the guy?" Jeremy said.

"The guy? What guy?" Manny said, maintaining his polite smile.

"You damn well know what guy. The one from the lounge who was almost killed by a bottle of whisky around the back of his head. That guy," Jeremy said, squaring up to Manny.

"I'm sorry, sir, but I wasn't there. What happened?"

"I've just told you, dammit! Some guy swung a bottle at a passenger and nearly killed him. Two of you guys carried him off down here with a towel pressed to the back of his head, covering the gaping wound. Why am I telling you this? Of course you know what happened." Jeremy was getting frustrated. "Now, where the hell is the guy and what is happening on this godforsaken ship?"

"Sir, you must be mistaken. There is no man down here," came another voice from behind the couple.

Jeremy swiftly turned around to see two more crew members directly behind him.

"I'm telling you there is. We followed you two down here with a guy—"

"James Duke," Christine added.

"—who had just had his head caved in by some jealous bastard in the lounge," Jeremy insisted.

"Surely if that was the case, sir, wouldn't we be covered in blood?" the other of the two crew members said.

Jeremy scanned both men and noticed not a single blemish on their pristine white jackets. With an inkling that this was going nowhere, plus it was three onto one, Jeremy decided it would be a prudent move to make a tactical retreat...for now.

"Christine, come on. We're going back on deck. We must have been mistaken," Jeremy said, and with Christine holding onto his arm, he turned and escorted her back to the stairs.

As he placed his foot on the first step. He paused and turned to the three men.

"Oh, and the captain?" he asked.

"Yes, sir. He is aware and he will see you soon. As soon as he—"

"Yes, I know. As soon as he's finished what he's doing," Jeremy finished what he thought was the constant lie from the entire staff.

Chapter 13

Jeremy escorted Christine up the stairs with resistance.

"What on earth are you doing? We should demand the truth. I thought you were a lawyer. Surely that's your job; to demand the truth," Christine protested.

Jeremy didn't reply.

Moments later, the couple reached the top. Jeremy looked around to make sure they were alone and turned to Christine.

"Sometimes going headlong into battle is not the most productive way. Ever heard of the saying 'softly, softly'?"

A puzzled, furrowed brow was Christine's reply.

"No, of course you haven't. 'Softly, softly, catchee monkey'?" Jeremy said, with an air of frustration.

"Ah, I've heard of that. Isn't it something to do with stealth?" Christine said, smiling.

"Close enough. Look, we both know something isn't right here and for whatever reason the three stooges down there, along with every other goddam Manny, refuse to tell us what's going on." Jeremy looked around again, ensuring privacy. "So, we'll find the proof ourselves. It's not a big ship, it can't be that difficult to find. That son of a bitch, Captain Obol, can't be far away either."

Jeremy looked out into the millpond of a sea. A cool breeze from the bow confirmed they were travelling forward. Not that there was any noise to confirm this. Surely there should have been stronger sounding waves lapping against the sides of the ship? It was quiet enough for them to hear at least that. Not a cloud in the sky and with the moon still hanging over the starboard side, a thought suddenly struck him.

"Goddamn lying bastards. That's what was wrong." Jeremy said, tapping his forehead with the palm of his hand.

Christine looked at him.

"What?"

"The lying bastards." Jeremy looked at her and pointed out to sea. "They said we were sailing south, right? Well, the moon rises in the east and sets in the west," he explained.

Christine wasn't good with directions and this information meant nothing to her.

"If we are sailing south, then north is that way." Jeremy pointed to the rear of the ship. "And that means that this side is east."

"OK?" Christine said, not sure what Jeremy was getting at.

"Jesus, didn't you learn anything at school? If this side is east and the moon rises in the east, then why the hell is it rising in the west? Assuming that we're heading south? We have to be heading north for the moon to rise on the other side of the ship."

"So why did they lie and tell us we were going south?" Christine asked.

"Exactly. The moon doesn't rise in the west. Why are those bastards lying and where the hell are we actually going? Look, let's go back to the bar and figure out where to go next."

With a nod of a head, Christine took the lead and headed back. As they reached the lounge windows, she stopped.

"How the hell is that possible?" she said as she looked into the bar.

Jeremy looked inside to see what she had seen.

"It's not. Not possible at all," he muttered.

James Duke was sitting at the bar with a young woman by his side. The same man whom the cabin crew had carried off only minutes earlier, having had a bottle broken over the back of his head. Through the window, the couple saw him roll his sleeve up and showing the woman his watch.

"Is this the same man?" Christine said, not taking her eyes off James.

"One way to find out," Jeremy said, who opened the lounge door and went in.

Chapter 14

"Back again Mr Leadstone? Miss Sommers," the bartender smiled.

Jeremy ignored the greeting and walked over to James. Standing in front of the seated couple, Jeremy looked at James, creating an awkward situation for the lothario. James stopped chatting and looked at the man, who had just halted his flow.

"Can I help you?" James said, looking up at the unwanted man.

"You OK?" Jeremy asked with a demanding tone.

"Why wouldn't I be? I'd be better, though, if you left us alone. We're having a private chat, if you don't mind," James said, looking annoyed.

Jeremy looked at James with a firm gaze, and then at the young woman. It was definitely the right man. He hadn't dreamt it, nor had he got the wrong man. This man only minutes ago should have been fighting for his life, yet here he was, lusting over a young woman. He then recognised the young woman. It was the same woman who James had been chatting to, so again, why wasn't she covered in glass and whisky?

"That was a polite way to say, go away. Would you like it in a clearer tone?" James said, waiting for this stranger to leave.

"Yes, sorry. My mistake. I thought you were someone else. Have a good evening." Jeremy apologised.

Jeremy backed away. As he looked around, he noticed Christine had found a table and was being attended to by a waiter. As the waiter left the table, Jeremy went and sat down across the table from her.

"That not only is the same guy—"

"James Duke," Christine interrupted.

"Yes, whatever, but that's the same woman. When I approached him, he acted like nothing had happened," Jeremy said.

"How is that possible? I mean, there's no glass anywhere, there's no blood and everybody is acting like nothing's happened," Christine said, looking around the lounge. "Look! There's that guy eyeing up James."

Jeremy recognised the fire in the man's eyes and knew what was coming next.

"Why don't you go over to him and chat to him for a short while. I'll go back over to Marianne over there and see if she knows me," he said.

With a nod, Christine got up and made her way over to the man. Just as Jeremy was getting up himself, he heard Christine say hello and ask if she could sit with him. With her looks, she could easily distract the man.

"Marianne? May I sit?" Jeremy said to the woman who was finishing a platter of whatever had been in front of her.

"Hi, doll. Of course you can," Marianne smiled with the left side of mouth full of food.

'Thank God she remembers me,' thought Jeremy.

"How's it going?" Jeremy said, as he took a seat opposite the woman. "Hey what about earlier on? That was a sight, wasn't it?"

A faint smile came over Marianne's face. Jeremy saw right away that she had not a clue what he was talking about. Quickly thinking, he continued.

"Yes, that shooting star was amazing. Did you see it?"

"Sorry, I didn't. I've been in here all evening. You ought to try the crab, it's *to die* for, doll. How did you know my name? And you are?" Marianne asked.

"Sorry, I'm Jeremy. And apologies for being a little forward, using your first name, but I heard you talking to Manny, and I picked it up from your chat with him. Hope you don't mind."

Marianne didn't recall mentioning her name, but figured she must have done as she chatted to the lovely Manny.

"It's OK, doll. So how you finding this cruise? I go on so many but the food on here is just out of this world," Marianne replied.

Jeremy was losing things to talk about. He had found out what he needed to. No one had seen the attack on James even though it was only minutes ago and no way had the crew enough time to clean up and brainwash everyone into forgetting it. The bone splitting crash was enough to be etched into everyone's minds.

"Oh, it's great. I love cruises. My wife and I go on so many," Jeremy said, feigning interest.

Marianne looked over at Christine, who was chatting with another man at the opposite of the bar. With a raised eyebrow, Marianne turned back to Jeremy and replied.

"So I see. Hey who am I to judge."

Quickly picking up what the woman had seen, Jeremy felt he had to defend himself.

"Oh, she's not my wife, just someone I met on here," Jeremy realised that his last comment hadn't helped his situation at all. "Dammit, no! I don't know that woman, well, not like that. She is just helping me with a problem."

"I'm sure she is...I had a pair like that, one time, when I was much younger, however mine were real. And not that you'd believe me now, but I had a body like that too," Marianne said, eyeing Christine's cleavage and body.

That was the second time Marianne had told him that and he still doubted that, but went along with it, anyway. He had to get away from the situation before this large elderly woman tried her luck with him.

'That's if she could steer away from the food first,' he thought.

"I'm sure you did, anyway it's been nice speaking with you, Marianne. Maybe we can meet up when we dock at—?"

Jeremy left the sentence in the air for the woman to finish, and hopefully mention where that may be.

"Sure doll. I'll look forward to it," she said as she eyed his chest from his Adam's apple down to the tabletop.

Jeremy got up, smiled and wandered back to his table, feeling Marianne's eyes burning a hole into the seat of his trousers.

Chapter 15

"Hi, my name is Christine. What's yours?" Christine said as the man broke his gaze from the bar area and settled on her chest.

"It's Stephen, Stephen Hibbert. Pleased to meet you," he replied.

A clammy hand reached out over the table to greet the young busty woman. Christine shivered inside as she took hold of the outstretched hand. One thing she hated was a limp hand and a clammy one at that. Her smile was hiding a curled lip of revulsion, but she knew she had to do something.

"So, how you enjoying the trip?" she enquired.

Stephen looked up at the bar at the older man, who was draping himself over the young woman, and sneered.

"I'm enjoying it, thanks, but there're guys like *him* who make my blood boil." Stephen said with a venomous tone.

Stephen Hibbert was an average man in his early forties who had no redeeming features. With thinning, frizzy hair that was going grey, Stephen was the type of man you could easily pass by in the street and not even notice.

Christine glanced down at the whisky bottle on the table and then turned to face the bar, knowing exactly who he was staring at.

"Oh him? Don't pay any attention to him. He's not worth it. You know, he tried it on with me when I first came in here. I quickly told him where to go." Christine said with a dismissive smile.

Stephen looked at her strangely.

"I've been here all night, and this is the first time you've come in. Are you trying to scam me?" he demanded.

Christine could feel the tension rising over the table and had to think on her feet.

"No, I'm not scamming you. Yesterday when I came in. You weren't here then. God, he was such a creep. And that watch of his...? Fake."

Stephen could not remember being on the ship the day before and really had not a clue how he'd got on board that evening. He definitely would not tell this busty blonde woman that though, as she may think he was some sort of mental case.

"Oh, Oh that's right. I wasn't in last night. I, err, was...in my room. Sorry, my bad, I thought you meant this evening," he replied.

Christine was back on the winning side.

"So, this guy. D'you know him?" she said, nodding over at the bar.

"No, but I've seen his kind before. Those slimy bastards, always getting the girls through their bullshit. Makes me so angry seeing them win at everything. Why don't she see this asshole for what he is? I'm getting fed up with everything going his way. The lucky bastard."

The last few words seemed to be spat out.

"No, I don't think so. If he was that lucky, he'd have a real Rolex and the shirt would be a good quality cotton one. Not the polyester supermarket rag it is. The man is just one great lie. He's not worth fretting over. And that girl?" Christine looked back at James' companion. "If she doesn't realise how fake he is, then more fool her."

Stephen still glared at him and the sickly patter he was giving the young woman. Christine felt she was winning, but then Stephen then took a deep breath and stood up. He picked up the whisky bottle, corked it and with it still in his hand, he made his way to the bar. Christine panicked. Her pep talk hadn't worked.

"Manny? Look after this, will you?" Stephen placed the bottle on the bar next to James. "Miss? This guy is a slime-ball and wants nothing from you but to get you into his bed as another notch on his bedpost. He's a loser, and that isn't even a real Rolex. It's just like the wearer. Fake." Stephen glared at James and returned to face the young woman. "Don't do anything stupid, as you may catch something you really don't want."

With a casual salute to the young woman and a glare at James, Stephen walked out of the lounge, leaving James knowing he had found him out.

Christine watched as Stephen belittled the lecherous man and as he left, the young woman climbed down from her bar stool and wandered over to an empty table. James looked at the nearly empty whisky bottle and took it before the bartender could shelve it.

"I'll have that thanks, Manny."

James uncorked the bottle, raised it and took a large slug of whisky, wincing as he swallowed the firewater.

With a sigh of relief, Christine dropped her head, knowing she had just stopped a nasty incident from taking place. Briefly relishing the victory, she raised her head, scanning the lounge for Jeremy, who was sitting on the table they had been at when they walked in. He saw Christine and gave a slight, approving smile and nod of the head. Moments later, she was sitting back with him and recounting what they had said.

"It's like this never happened and that we've changed what could've been," Christine said, feeling proud of her actions.

"We both know it happened, as we both can't imagine the same thing, but it's like we were never here. When I first approached—um—James, he didn't recognise me, even though I'd shown him up earlier for the fraud that he was. Then, going over to chat to Marianne, she didn't know me either."

Jeremy looked around the lounge, hoping to find something that made sense.

"Are we actually here? Is this just a dream?" he said to himself.

Christine smiled.

"If this is a dream, you best not call my name out or else you've some explaining to do with your wife when you wake." Christine giggled.

For a moment, Jeremy found the funny side of what Christine had said and smiled.

"God knows what she'd do if I called your name out," Jeremy said. "Probably shoot me, if she had the guts...or a gun."

The loud bang and sharp pain returned to Jeremy, and he grabbed his chest. This time, he also heard what sounded like a distant shout or scream.

'What the hell is it?' he thought. 'I've never felt like this before.'

"Oh, there's something definitely wrong with you. Are you going to die on me?" Christine said, who had seen her friend wince again.

"No, I'm fine. I promise. I'm not going to die on you," Jeremy said, trying to raise a smile.

'I knew a man who died on a young woman, in flagrante, but that's a story not for your ears,' he thought as he looked at his companion.

"Look, we'll go out on deck. The fresh air will do the trick. Let's take a walk," he reassured her and walked to the exit.

Chapter 16

Jeremy looked out over the sea at the darkening sky and took a deep breath to quell the pain in his chest. What the hell was that voice doing in his head and whilst it sounded familiar, he just couldn't place it. Christine followed him out and stood by his side, trying to see what he was looking at. Or was it one of those reflective moments that men his age have when facing a potential heart attack. Jeremy broke the silence without looking at her.

"North. Not south. Lying bastard, whatever his goddamn name is. I knew there was something wrong with the moon," he muttered.

Christine looked up at him.

"I don't understand. Why did he tell us we were heading south? What benefit would he get from that?"

Jeremy thought that was a good point.

"Don't know, but I'm sure we can ask him next time we see him. We can also ask for his real name, too. If we ever get off this godforsaken ship, I will sue the company for everything I can. Lying bastards. Come on. Let's get some air and think about what we're going to do next."

The couple walked steadily along the deck towards the rear of the ship, enjoying the silence and mild breeze as they sailed through the evening. As they reached the stern, Christine was the first to see Stephen leaning on the balustrade and looking out to sea at the rear.

"Hi Stephen. How you feeling now?" she called out.

Stephen didn't answer.

Not wanting to witness another troubled man take his life, Christine hastened her pace and joined him.

"Are you OK? You seemed a little upset back there," she asked.

Stephen didn't reply but looked down at the base of the ship where it met the water. Jeremy joined the couple and again enquired what was wrong.

Eventually, Stephen replied cryptically.

"The sea."

His companions looked at each other, nonplussed by what that meant.

"I'm sorry Stephen. What about the sea?" Jeremy said.

"Look at it," was the reply.

Jeremy leaned over to peer into the dark waters below, gripping hold of the balustrade. A quick glance did not give any answer.

"What about it?" Jeremy said, looking puzzled at Christine.

"Just look at it. Spot anything wrong?" Stephen said, still gazing into the inky blackness.

Jeremy, thinking there had to be something wrong and whatever it was he had not seen it on his first glance, leaned over for a further look. 'If a man can disappear in the sea without a sound, then something could well be wrong,' he thought, examining the sea. It then struck him.

"How is this possible?" he whispered.

Christine looked at him and at Stephen, then joined them, looking over the side of the ship.

"What? What is it? I can't see anything," she said.

Jeremy stood upright and looked at her.

"Stand up. Do you feel anything?" he said.

Christine did as she was asked.

"No. Only a breeze on the side of my face."

"That'll be the wind as we're sailing along, won't it?" Jeremy said.

"I would think so," Christine said, not sure where this was going.

"So, if we're moving forward and you're noticing the breeze, then what would you expect to see if you looked over the back of the ship?" Jeremy continued.

Christine looked again for several seconds and came back up with frustration on her face.

"OK, I know you can see something and you're going to tease me and say something like 'how can you not see it!'. But I'm not a sharp-eyed lawyer like you, so why don't you tell me and put me out of this misery.

Jesus! I so hate smartass men who do this sort of thing."

Jeremy felt her anger and understood that men had subjected her to this behaviour for some time. So calmly, and with the least patronising tone he could muster, he replied.

"You're not what you think. I didn't mean for it to sound that way, but...here." Jeremy leaned over again. "Look...it took me a second or two to work it out. Stephen is right. If we are moving forward, then one thing you should see at the back of a ship is...waves. The wake of the water, moving as we sail through it. But look; nothing. It's as though we're standing still."

Christine looked over and saw what the others did. Standing upright and looking towards the front of the ship to feel the breeze on her face, then back over the edge.

"Holy shit! How is that happening?"

"I really couldn't tell you. I'm feeling a little uneasy about this whole thing," Jeremy said.

He hadn't felt this uneasy since he was a fresh-faced lawyer in a high-profile case and was, at one point, losing.

"Let's go to the front and make sure we are actually moving and it's not just the wind making us think we're moving," she said as she grabbed Jeremy's hand making her way to the other side of the ship and towards the bow.

"Hang on," Stephen said. "I'm coming too. I want to find out what's going on as well."

All three made their way along the deck until they reached Marcus, who had fallen into a light sleep. As they approached, the sound of their feet on the deck awoke him and he looked over at them.

"Hey. How's it going?" he called out, with a casual wave.

"Marcus, there's something very wrong with the ship. I can't explain, but we need to either find out what's going on or get off quickly," Jeremy explained.

Marcus displayed a perplexed, raised eyebrow.

"OK dude. Hey, how d'you know my name? Have we met?"

The question halted Jeremy and Christine. Whilst she met him briefly, she thought that she should have had much more of an impact on this slob. Jeremy had spoken to this man for much longer and surely should have recognised him. Yet here he was, asking such a question.

"Marcus. We were only talking less than an hour ago. Remember? I asked you how we got on this ship and where it was going? You even ordered some cheesy puffs and a soda," Jeremy said.

"Well, I ordered the stuff, that's for sure, but I don't remember you. Sorry, dude."

As Marcus looked up at the strangers, Jeremy concluded that whatever had happened down below deck and with everyone in the bar going back to as it was before Stephen hit the guy, it wasn't just the bar folk who had been brainwashed.

"Hey, fella. I'm sorry to have bothered you. Our mistake," Jeremy said with a resigned smile.

"Nah! No problem, dude," Marcus said, who picked up a bag that was by his side and delved in for another handful of cheesy puffs.

"Come on, you two, I'll explain in a minute," Jeremy said as he walked away.

Chapter 17

Jeremy, Christine, and Stephen had walked a short distance along the ship and out of earshot from the recumbent Marcus, when Jeremy stopped.

"Stephen. You noticed that the sea was not moving at the back of the ship, right? Well, there's been other things going amiss on here too," Jeremy said.

"Like?" Stephen asked, looking at Jeremy.

"Earlier, when Christine approached you and chatted to you? Well, that wasn't the first time we'd seen you. Not long before that, we were all in the bar when the guy who was chatting with that young woman was attacked." Jeremy continued.

"Bullshit! I'd been there all evening and I would have seen that asshole getting what he deserved," Stephen snapped.

"It's true, Stephen," Christine added. "In fact, it was you who attacked him. With your whisky bottle."

"Bullshit! Are you guys winding me up as it's not funny if you are," Stephen said, feeling defensive and a little vulnerable.

"Sorry, but it's true," Jeremy said. "The same asshole accosted Christine when I approached him up and showed him up over the fake Rolex. A goddamn Rolex

Seamaster, for Christ's sake," Jeremy broke a smile over the ridiculousness of the fake and continued.

"We had sat down at a table when we saw you walk over and break the bottle over his head. He should have died with the force you used, but some waiters dragged you off him and more carted him off downstairs.

They carried him out of there and took him below deck. We followed them downstairs, but when we got there, it was weird. It was like an old Spanish Galleon. Old gnarled wood panels. More cabin crew stopped us and basically told us to stop poking our noses into their business, so we left.

When we got back into the bar, there you were, glaring at the same guy who hadn't a scratch on him. No blood, nothing. No one in the lounge knew of anything happening. Christine went over to talk you out of doing it again, which you did, thank God.

It seems someone hit rewind and made it appear like it never happened. And the thing with Marcus? When I first woke up on this ship, he was next to me and we chatted for a short while. Again, he didn't recognise me. It's all weird, but they're the facts, I can assure you of that." Jeremy said with his usual court room tone in his voice.

Stephen looked at Jeremy and noticed that this man wasn't joking. He tried to figure out what he had just been told and was failing drastically.

"Listen," Jeremy continued. "Do you remember how you got here? Where, or when, did you board? Do you know where you're going?"

Stephen glanced down and pondered over this for a second. Before he could answer, Jeremy continued.

"No, neither do we. I asked one of the 'Manny' waiters. They're all called Manny by the way, and they said we were sailing south, but if we were, then the moon would have been rising in the east, which it just doesn't do.

We saw a guy jump to his death over the back of the ship but with no splash, and when the crew, who were there, saw this, they ushered us away and did nothing! We all then see that the ship's stern isn't casting a wake as it goes through the sea. So you think slugging that asshole with your whisky bottle is bullshit?"

Stephen and Christine were silent as they tried to absorb all the information Jeremy had just divulged.

"Shit! What the hell is this place?" Stephen said, as he glanced at the other two, hoping for an answer.

"A good question. One of which we don't have an answer to...yet," Jeremy assured him.

Looking along the deck towards the bow, Jeremy spied another stairway.

"Here, we'll show you what it's like down there."

The group made their way to the stairs and, after a brief check to make sure the coast was clear, they quietly descended.

"Can I have your cell again, Christine?" Jeremy asked, as they reached the bottom.

The air was dank, and they heard creaking old, damp wood. With a click, the cell phone's torch sprung into life, lighting everything in front of it. Panning across the darkness, the white LED light exposed the glistening wooden planks of an old ship's hull. Puddles of water underfoot reflected ripples on the legs of each person.

"Oh, Christ!" Stephen gazed around as the sights unfolded in front of him. "What the hell is that smell?"

As an owner of a successful law firm, it had been a while since Jeremy had been 'out in the field'. As a beginner, he had visited crime scenes and hospital morgues for evidential purposes, and that smell would be in his memory banks for all eternity.

"I think we ought to leave...now!" Jeremy said with some urgency.

"What is it?" Christine said, worried by the tone of Jeremy's voice.

"I'll tell you when we get out, but we need to go now!"

Chapter 18

Hastily making their way out, with a sense of fear rising within each person, they reached the open deck and fresh air.

"What was that smell?" Stephen asked.

"Death," Jeremy said, not wanting to sugar coat his reply. "Believe me, I've been in many situations where death surrounds you and it's something you never forget. I don't know who's died, but I sure as hell don't want to stumble across some cadaver on this godforsaken ship. I also think neither of you would relish that experience. This place is weird enough as it is and I've enough to process without tripping over some rotting corpse."

Christine wretched as she held back the surge of vomit from deep inside.

"I've seen death," Stephen said coldly.

The two others looked at each other, then at the man in front of them.

Stephen began his solemn confession.

"I had a real estate company with my friend and business partner, Derek. Derek Holmes. It was doing very well indeed. We had most of the mid-west under our belts. Franchises all over the place. We had everything we could ever want. Well, Derek did. He married this beautiful woman called Sophie. Honestly, she was stunning. You ought to have seen her. I would have done anything for her."

Jeremy had heard similar stories before and had a good idea what was coming next.

"I knew Derek was having affairs everywhere. If it wasn't the vendors, it was the prospective buyers. He just couldn't keep it in his pants. And here was this beautiful woman who was suffering while her bastard of a husband played away.

This one evening, Derek had gone off to visit one of his whores under the guise of going to a seminar for the weekend whilst I worked in the office on our tax returns. The IRS are bastards with folk like us and I had to make sure the books were up to date before passing them to our accountant.

Whilst he played God knows what, and possibly catching something very nasty, I worked my ass off in the office. This one night, Sophie came to the office. We chatted for hours, but it seemed like seconds. After half a bottle of whisky, one thing led to another and the next thing I know, in a blink of an eye, we were naked. Clearing Derek's desk of all his clutter so we could, well, you know.

Months passed, and it turned out that Sophie knew about Derek's extra-marital activities and had grown fed up with his infidelities. She convinced me that both the company and I would be better off without him. Plus, there would be nothing stopping us from being together then.

She had this plan to get rid of Derek permanently, and it involved me. It was purely for our benefit, she claimed, and it was a foolproof plan. So—" Stephen gave a nonchalant shrug. "I went through with it. I can still remember what I did and how he looked afterwards. I can't believe I did that to my friend, but...I did it. I'll never forget the sound of the gun going off in my hand. God, it was loud. I've never held a gun before. Those things are heavy, you know. I didn't realise how realistic the movies are these days with the brain matter and blood. Jesus, it was everywhere.

The company was now mine. Well, ours. It wasn't long before me and Sophie moved in together and things started off well. 'Hibbert's Holmes' was doing great, better now without Casanova messing things up. Then I had to do more work, the work Derek would have done. Sophie didn't like that to start off with, but then she got used to it.

She started spending more time at the gym, and whilst she looked good because of it, she was always tired and went to bed early. Anyway, it was my birthday recently, and I figured Sophie bought me this trip as a gift for all the work I did. God knows I needed it. My brain was mush after all that work and even now I'm struggling to remember how I got here."

Stephen inhaled and breathed a sigh of relief as he confessed his sins and washed away his guilt.

"Anyway, there's one less asshole in the world. Isn't that one of those seven deadly sins or something that I committed? Coveting your neighbour's wife? Mind you, I think Derek coveted everyone's wives."

Jeremy was about to correct him as it was one of the ten commandments not of the deadly sins, but then realised that he had been guilty of the same. There had been so many affairs, yet Joanna had never spotted a single one.

'God, I'm good,' he thought.

Just at the back of his mind, he heard a voice, angry and upset. Jeremy was good at listening to those voices, as they always gave him the right path to go down. This one, however, was an unfamiliar voice. One that did not give him a feeling of superiority, but a sense of sadness.

'Am I feeling guilty? Of what?' Jeremy shook his head as if to rid him of the thought.

"Well. Didn't see that coming!" Christine said, having heard the confession. "I know what you mean, though. I've been on the other end of men like that. They promise the world when, in reality, all they give you is a damp patch in bed and a guilty feeling when you find out that they're married. The bastards never tell you they are, though. Or when they do, it's always, 'my wife doesn't understand or we're about to get separated'. Either line is pure bull."

Jeremy looked at Christine with fresh eyes. She had, in all appearances, come across as some blonde bimbo who cared more about her looks than anything or anyone else. However, her looks came at a cost, more than just a monetary one.

"OK, Stephen. Feel better for that?" Jeremy said.

"Not as much as I thought I would. I don't even know why I told you that," he replied.

Christine broke the awkward silence.

"In the meantime, here we are, on a ship that looks like another ship and smells of death!"

Reality came crashing back. Jeremy scanned the deck for inspiration. 'Which way to go?' Near the bow was a stairway leading up.

"OK. If below smells of death and looks like the Marie Celeste, let's see what up top looks like."

Chapter 19

Jeremy jogged the few paces to the stairs, leading the way, with the other two following. With no sign of the crew in the area, Jeremy looked up and climbed the stairs. With all three reaching the top, they looked in awe at the covered decking which led towards several cabin doors. None of the lights were on in any cabin. Jeremy tried the first door and found it unlocked.

"Hello? Anyone here?" Jeremy called as he opened the door and peered in.

With no answer from the pitch black room, a quick fumble next to the door frame and Jeremy found the light switch. Several ornate light fittings illuminated the place as he flicked the switch, much to the amazement of all three.

At the entrance to the cabin, a marble-floored hallway beckoned them into an awaiting lounge and bedroom area. An emperor size bed festooned with luxury linens tussled with the couch for dominance over the cabin. Both appeared immense and could have easily catered to a small family.

"Oh my God!" Christine said with a childlike shriek.

She pushed past Jeremy and launched herself, towards the enormous bed. As she landed, Christine sank into the plush quilted cover.

"Oh my God, guys. You really ought to try this. God, it's heavenly," Christine squealed, half covered with a quilt.

Stephen quickly glanced over at Jeremy and ran to the bed. Jeremy had noticed the sideward glance, and immediately recognised the meaning behind it. Whilst he was warming slightly towards Christine, he had no intention of getting into bed with her. Stephen, however, came across as if he was in a race with Jeremy, trying to beat him to it.

'What is wrong with this guy?' Jeremy thought. 'First, the envious stare at that asshole at the bar, where he broke his skull with the whisky bottle, and now this.'

Jeremy wandered further into the room. He looked around for something that identified the ship's owner or company, or any information that stated where they were heading. Plus, whose room was this? His two acquaintances obviously hadn't booked it because if they had, they wouldn't have been so overwhelmed at its opulence. A subtle but strange sensation came over Jeremy.

"When you two have finished messing up the bed, can we get back to what we came here for and to find out what on earth is happening?" Jeremy said as he sifted through the pamphlets on the nearby desk.

The two sat up on the bed, both out of breath after their cavorting. Christine's eyes sparkled, a look of joy etched on her face. Stephen, however, leered at Jeremy, which bewildered him a little.

Christine, shuffling to the edge on the bed and jumping off, hitched up her jeans, unknowingly giving Stephen an eye-level view of her enhanced rear.

"Jesus!" Stephen muttered at the sight of the taut denim jeans.

Christine turned to see Stephen staring and giggled at the thought of a man lusting after her.

"Jesus Christ. Just for one second, can you stop trying to get men to ogle you and try to help me find some information?" Jeremy demanded as he continued to search the cupboards and drawers.

"Oh, come on. What's your problem? Stephen wasn't doing any harm, and all I was doing was hitching my jeans up. There's no law against that, is there Mr Lawyer-man?" Christine remonstrated.

Jeremy stopped what he was doing and faced her with a growing unfamiliar anger.

"You feel fine being on this ship, even though you don't know how you got on here or where the hell we're going. I, on the other hand, don't feel fine. The cabin crew lie to us regarding where we're going. A man jumps to his death and the hull of the ship is rotting away. So forgive me if I have a little more urgency in finding out what the hell is happening," Jeremy said, his voice becoming rapidly stern as he spoke.

Christine had experience with how to respond to any man who thought he could talk to her like that and get away with it, and fired back.

"Listen here, you jerk. No, I don't know how I got on this boat, but yet here I am. Unlike you, I don't feel uncomfortable about being on here even though I've seen some scary sights and things that I cannot explain. Yes, it's spooked me and yes, I'm still crapping myself over the things we've seen, but you know what? Since coming into this room, I really don't care. We could be on a slow boat to China, but if we have luxury like this, then who gives a shit?"

"I do, goddammit!" Jeremy said, raising his voice. "You stay here with this loser wannabe if you like, but I'm going to find out just what the hell is going on."

Stephen got off the bed and approached Jeremy with anger in his eyes.

"Loser wannabe? Who the hell are you to call me that? You, jumped-up asshole. Just because I don't wear a fancy watch and wear expensive clothing like you, it doesn't mean I'm a loser. And I'm definitely not a wannabe! I own a company, just like you. I've met people like you. Constantly getting what they want and still wanting more. Nothing is ever enough for you, is it? More, more, more, that's all you want."

Stephen sneered at the man in front of him, glancing down at Jeremy's left hand, noticing his wedding ring.

"God, I pity your wife, living with a complete asshole like you. Something tells me you've made her life a living hell. Oh yes, a beautiful house with beautiful things, but what does it mean if the husband you love screws around and doesn't love you back? You think she doesn't know, but she will do. You always coming back from *'that meeting'* smelling of your secretary's perfume. Jesus, you make me sick. Why is it you guys can do whatever you want and think you can get away with it?"

Jeremy was taken aback by how accurate this man was, even though he had only met him minutes ago. The fighting lawyer in him then emerged. Squaring up to his attacker, Jeremy fired both barrels, not only at Stephen, but at Christine, too.

"You think you know me and my life when it's patently clear you have not a clue what I do or how hard I work. Do you think I built this company by just pissing around with the likes of you? I've had to fight hard for it and my wife knew exactly what she was taking on when I married her. Those meetings you talk about, *do* go on, and that's the price you pay for being the top of the tree. If I hadn't done what I did, then there'd be hundreds of people without a job. Do you think all that is easy...? Well? Do you...? You just see me and men like me living the highlife.

People like you always see the graceful swan and never the paddling webbed feet underneath. I have never met a more jealous man in my entire life. Christ, you'd be jealous if I took a shit. You'd have to do the same thing just to try to be the same as me. You are truly a pathetic little man with nothing in his life but envy. If it wasn't because I don't care about assholes like you, then I'd actually feel sorry for you."

Before Christine could challenge Jeremy over the barrage of insults, he turned on her.

"And you, you little whore. Is your life so pitiful that you have to make yourself into something that you clearly are not? With your fake tits and ass, you sicken me. What does the real Christine Sommers look like? Is she that ugly that she has to spend every dollar to make herself attractive? News flash honey. It's not working. Ever heard the quote 'you can't make a silk purse out of a sow's ear'? No, you probably haven't, as your intellect is lower than your hipster jeans. All you care about is your looks and nothing else. You pride yourself on your looks and how much you spend on plastic surgery—"

Before Jeremy could continue, a stinging sensation radiated from his left cheek to his entire face, as a right hand connected with his face. The slap from Christine stopped Jeremy in his tracks, and as he looked at her, he could see tears of rage streaming down her face.

"You bastard. How dare you! How dare you presume to know me? You've not a clue about me or what I've been through. Stephen was right about men like you. It's all about greed. The more you have, the more you want. But that's alright for you but for people like us? Oh no, people like us cannot try to improve ourselves without maggots like you trying to put us down. Do you honestly think that your wife doesn't see you for who you truly are? Men like you don't think women see right through you, but they do—"

As Christine said that, Jeremy saw a vision in his minds-eye; an image of Joanna with tears in her eyes and screaming at him. The indistinct voice he had heard earlier, prior to the bang and pain in his chest, was Joanna!

"Are you listening to me? Asshole!" Christine broke into Jeremy's thoughts. "Well, screw you. You can go on your own quest to find out shit. I don't care. I never really did. God, how stupid was I to worry about you and your heart attacks. I hope you drop dead. You called Stephen a loser, well maybe you should look in the mirror sometime." Christine's barrage of home truths ended in a broken voice as tears streamed down her face.

In all his years as an up-and-coming lawyer, a comeback line was something that Jeremy was never stuck for, yet here he was, up against some young woman whose only knowledge of a courtroom was gleaned from the television.

His mind was a whirlwind with what Christine had said and the pain in his chest, and a vague impression of Joanna looking upset. What was it he couldn't quite grasp? This young woman just handed him his ass on a plate. The sound of the loud bang resounded in Jeremy's mind and Joanna's tearful face. It was time to leave before Christine fired another blow.

"I'm out of here," Jeremy whispered, looking dazed.

Chapter 20

Stunned, and turning slowly for the door, he made his way out and into the cool night air. Quietly closing the door behind him, Jeremy looked out to sea through a window on the deck. As he stared at the sea, all that was in his line of sight was Joanna, with tears streaming down her face and his lack of emotion towards her. The sharp pain raced through his chest again, bringing him back to the deck of the ship. As he grabbed at his chest, Jeremy glimpsed his reflection in the window–it was covered in blood!

"What the?!"

Jeremy gasped, looked down at his chest, and saw nothing but his white shirt. He glanced up at his reflection and saw himself, uninjured, with no blood, just himself. The pain was subsiding but still present.

"Why was she so upset?" Jeremy muttered to himself. 'What had I done? Had I done something, or was it something else? Was it real or was it this goddamned ship? Why the hell did I have a go at Stephen and Christine? What the hell is happening to me?' he wondered.

Jeremy shook his head to rid himself of the questions and carry on with the fundamental questions; the where and how. Where was he? How did he get on board? And where was he going?

Jeremy turned towards the door of the cabin he had just exited. The deck was quiet. All he could hear was the crying of a woman from inside the cabin. He knew he had overstepped the mark by miles and no amount of apologising would make up for the hurtful things he said. Plus, he didn't want another ass whooping by an upset firecracker like Christine. The journey to find out his questions was his alone now.

Jeremy slowly walked to the rear of the deck, trying to work out what caused his sudden outburst. A short while later he reached the back of the ship which opened up revealing a pool surrounded by sun loungers.

"Hey! Hey fella!"

Jeremy looked over to the darker side of the pool and saw a man waving at him. 'Another helper,' Jeremy thought, so made his way over to him.

"Hey fella. This is gonna sound stupid, but where the hell am I?" the man said.

"Believe me when I say it doesn't sound stupid at all. I'm sorry, but I don't know. I can tell you we're on a ship and although the cabin crew tells us we're sailing south, they're lying. We're heading north. But where we set off from or our destination, your guess is as good as mine," Jeremy said.

"Bullshit! What the hell am I doing on a ship?" the man said, who had now stood. "Jesus. What a headache! You got any aspirin?" he said, holding the back of his head.

Jeremy looked at the man and could see by his clothing that there was no way a lowlife like this guy would ever set foot on a ship like this. 'His headache was probably through drinking too much cheap beer off the back of his pickup before driving home to beat up his wife,' he thought.

"Sorry, but it's true. I woke up a while ago, thinking the same as you. I don't remember getting on board and I've no idea where we're going. Do you remember what you were doing before now? Where were you? What were you doing?" Jeremy asked.

"What's with all the questions? You some sort of cop? If you are, then screw you. I've done nothing, so go harass someone else."

"Buddy, I'm not a cop, I'm a lawyer. I don't care what you've done, and you called me over, if you remember, so who's harassing who?"

The man stood toe to toe with Jeremy and stared into his eyes, breathing his stale beer breath from his nose onto Jeremy's top lip.

"You give me lip, boy, and I'll go to town on you; you'll wish you never met me," he growled.

Jeremy instantly sized up this man and although he was bigger and fitter than the lowlife in front of him, and could probably out manoeuvre him before he could even kiss his cousin, he tried a different tack.

"Sorry, but I'm having a terrible day. I woke up on the main deck, just below here," Jeremy pointed towards the balustrade. "I didn't know where I was or what I was doing here. I sure as hell didn't book this trip, and even if I did, it would have been with my wife, who isn't here. So I'm the same as you. I'm trying to find answers, but all I've found so far are more questions. I'm telling you, this ship is strange. Things are happening on here that I can't explain. Anyway, let's start again. I'm Jeremy."

The man looked at Jeremy as if weighing him up. Was he for real or was he just spinning him a yarn, thinking he was better than him.

"Jeremy? What sort of name is that? You a fag? Jeremy?" the man mocked.

"No, I'm not and it's the name my parents gave me, so I really don't have any option," Jeremy replied as he looked away from this man.

'You goddamned red neck piece of shit. Did I really defend homophobic assholes like you when I first started?' he thought to himself.

"There's no need to ask the cabin crew where you're going as they lie about the direction. They say we're going south, but if that's the case—"

"Then why is the moon rising in the west?" said the man. "Yeah, I can see. Don't think that just because I don't wear a suit that don't mean I'm stupid."

"So what's your name?" Jeremy said, trying not to show his revulsion for this poor excuse of a man.

"Bobby. You can call me Bobby."

"OK, Bobby. So, do you remember where you were just before you woke up?"

"I was sleeping, of course, dumbass."

Jeremy bit his tongue. The lack of Bobby's intelligence was getting frustrating but surrendering to his annoyance would not get him anywhere. He had to get as much information out of this imbecile as possible.

"OK. Before that."

"I don't know," Bobby said, rubbing the back of his head. "Jeez, my head hurts. All I remember is waking up here and this goddam headache. Did I ask you for aspirin?"

"Yes, you did and I'm sorry I don't have any," Jeremy said.

Jeremy, looking at Bobby, guessed he was about five-foot-ten-inch tall with a muscular body. He obviously did manual labour for a living; his physique and callused hands attested to that.

The swollen knuckles showed he wasn't shy in a bar-room brawl. He wore faded loose jeans and a dirty white T-shirt with the slogan 'Let's make America great again.' across the chest. Jeremy summed him up in one word - 'Loser'. If he had two words, then it would be 'Angry loser'.

By his unshaven appearance, Bobby cared less about his appearance than he did about the rest of humanity, but only just. His dislike for anything other than like-minded people was more than apparent.

"So what good are you then?" Bobby sneered.

"What is your problem?" Jeremy stood his ground. "I'm in the same situation as you, but whilst I've come over to see if we could help each other in finding answers to questions we both have, all you do is show hostility. OK, find out for yourself. I'm not standing around being subjected to your bullshit."

Jeremy turned and walked away.

"OK, OK. Look, I just don't know where I am. I got this goddam headache and if I find the son of a bitch who sucker-punched me, I'll kill the bastard. I ain't complicated but sometimes folk misunderstand me," Bobby said with a resigned tone.

Jeremy had heard this tone so many times before in his career. It usually meant that his client was a complete ass and was trying to bullshit his way out of a sticky situation that he needed to escape from.

Jeremy stopped and sat down on the edge of a nearby sun lounger.

"Right, Bobby. Sit down. Let's see if we can work out what's happened to you."

Bobby sat down facing Jeremy, with a lounger in between them, like a table. Locking his fingers and looking down at his feet, Bobby took an intake of breath.

"OK, Mr Lawyer-man. What do you want to hear?"

Jeremy was confident he was making headway. At least he had got this redneck off his high horse and now he could work on him to get information. Anything may help him find out what had happened, not just to Bobby but both of them.

"OK," Jeremy said. "Close your eyes and try to imagine the last thing you were doing before waking up here."

Bobby closed his eyes tightly, scrunching his face up.

"Just relax, Bobby. Relax and let the images come to you."

Bobby relaxed his eyelids and tried to recall what had happened.

"It was raining!" he said. "I remember it was raining...I think. Jeez my head. What in the devil's ass! I'm definitely warm. Hot even. Can feel sweat down the back of my neck. Yeah, that's right. I'm probably dehydrated. I've seen those adverts on the TV saying all that horseshit about these drinks you should take...yes, sir, I bet it's that dehydration. I remember feeling sweat on my neck and wiping it away...that's it. I wake up and I'm here. So what does that tell you, Lawyer-man?"

Bobby opened his eyes and looked at Jeremy. After some thinking, Jeremy shrugged his shoulders.

"Where do you live?"

"Montgomery, Alabama." Bobby said.

Jeremy thought for a second.

"The nearest beach is Pensacola, right? About a hundred to two hundred miles?"

"About that. I've never been, but I'd say so," Bobby said, who tried to sound intelligent but hadn't a clue as to the distance.

"So it's raining, you think. It's warm and your sweating. You are dehydrated and you wake up on a ship, and the nearest beach is one to two hundred miles away. And you don't have a clue how you got here."

"Sounds about right," Bobby nodded.

"Now, I'm only asking. I don't mean any offence, but do you take drugs?" Jeremy asked, raising his hands defensively.

"No sir, I do not. Just beer and weed."

Jeremy glossed over the response and ignored that last part.

"I don't know if you won a competition, anything like that or anyone of your buddies who plays pranks, but I can only imagine you had your beer spiked and maybe they put you on here as a prank?"

A shake of Bobby's head ruled out the possibilities suggested.

"No, not possible. I don't know anyone who would punk me, let alone have the cash for it. Plus, you're looking at a four-hour journey just to the ocean, so unless they injected me with a shitload of ketamine, then there's no way they could do it...Oh! I remember headlights! Does that mean anything?"

"Well, it might do. We've just got to work out what it could mean."

Bobby sat bolt upright.

"Well, you're the one with the brains. Work it out then."

"Bobby, I'm trying to. I don't even know how *I* got here. While you see headlights and rain, I feel a pain in my chest and a loud noise, then I think I see my wife crying and screaming. Why is she crying? What is she screaming about? And this pain in my chest is like something I've never felt before. Is it a heart attack? I don't know. Whatever it is, it hurts like hell."

Jeremy stood up and looked around the pool area, then up to the night sky.

"I'm going to see if I can find some answers. You coming?"

Bobby shrugged his shoulders.

"Hell. Why not?"

The two men briefly glanced around the pool area for any crew members and made their way along the left side of the ship. As they approached the first cabin door, Bobby tried the door handle and found it unlocked.

"What's say we go and have a look-see?" he said as he turned to Jeremy.

Jeremy had a strange feeling about entering another cabin. He vividly recalled going into the other room only minutes earlier, and the uneasy feeling it gave him.

That experience turned out to be a nightmare; arguing with two people he had previously partnered up with on the ship. Both were better than the redneck he had now come across.

"Just be careful going in," Jeremy warned Bobby. "There's something about these rooms that makes people go all...different."

Bobby smiled at Jeremy as he twisted the door handle.

"Man, anyone gets aggressive with me and I'll rip their head off and cram it up their ass."

Bobby opened the door and looked inside.

"What the hell?"

"What? What is it?" Jeremy asked just as Bobby flicked the light switch.

"Jesus! I don't believe it!" Bobby flicked the switch again and turn the lights off. "This shit just gets weirder!"

Jeremy stepped closer to the cabin door and looked inside.

In the dark, Jeremy couldn't see anything straight away until his eyes got accustomed to the darkness.

"See anything?" Bobby said to Jeremy as he peered in and waited for a response.

As the pupils of Jeremy's eyes widened to see inside, he noticed that the room was just like the lower deck, empty, old and gnarly with creaking timbers as if on a galleon or similar.

"Now watch," Bobby said as he flicked the light switch back on.

Light instantly bathed the room. Table lamps and ceiling lights lit up the opulent room and a fresh smell of newly cleaned cabin wafted Jeremy's way.

An enormous bed struggled for attention and was fighting against the large couch, coffee table, and drinks bar - similar to the last one. The walls were painted in a creamy white, with a slight pearlescent hue. The twill of the carpet was thick enough that you could easily lose your feet in. Everything about the room just screamed 'expensive'. Bobby then turned the lights back off.

A slowly emerging scene of a wooden room replaced the instant blackness along with a musty aroma of ancient damp wood. Bobby flicked the switch again and instantly the room changed back into the luxurious cabin. Bobby glanced over at Jeremy and returned his gaze to the room.

"Now you explain this, Mr Lawyer-man."

As the two men stood in the cabin's doorway—both not wanting to enter—Jeremy shook his head. He was at a loss how or why this could be. None of this made any sense. He was either on a luxury yacht or some old tug boat from the 1920s. He first thought that he had probably been seeing things when he was downstairs on the lower deck, but seeing the room change as it did, confirmed that it was no illusion. Or not one that he could explain, anyway.

Both men stood in silence as they looked inside the cabin.

"I don't know what is going on here or how this can be," Jeremy broke the silence. "It just isn't possible."

Bobby flicked the lights off and the empty wooden room returned.

"Well, possible or not, Mr Lawyer-man, it's what I can see and unless some jackass is going to stand in front of me and pull a rabbit out of a top hat, I can only say that this is real. It ain't no magic show."

Bobby looked at Jeremy with a gaze that demanded an explanation.

"I honestly don't know." Jeremy stared into the dark room. "I just can't see how this is possible. It shouldn't be possible, but here it is. I just don't understand any of this. What sort of ship are we on?" Jeremy's voice faded out as he continued to stare inside the room.

The sudden sharp pain raced through the man's chest again with the screams of a woman. Joanna's sobbing face was clear in his mind as the searing pain enveloped his entire torso. The pain was becoming more intense as the evening wore on to a point where Jeremy's knees buckled and he fell to the floor.

"The hell is wrong with you? You having a heart attack?" Bobby said as he looked down at Jeremy, who was on his hands and knees, groaning with the pain.

"Jesus! What the hell is wrong with me?" Jeremy muttered to himself as a flash of Joanna's sobbing face looked down at him, calling him a bastard.

"You ok lawyer?" Bobby was a little more concerned than he intended to show. "Come on. Get up. We've got to find out what's happening. Can't be dicking around here all night."

With a helping hand under the Jeremy's arm, Bobby lifted the man up.

"There you go. Just walk it off. You'll be fine," Bobby said, reassuringly.

Jeremy took a moment to come to his senses and quickly closed the cabin door. Whatever was in the room to cause such an illusion was also not good for his health.

Looking over the port side of the ship and taking in a huge lungful of air, Jeremy pulled himself together and made the decision that they should move on and see if they could find the illusive Captain Obol.

"Come on. We need to find the captain. No one else seems to want to help us or give answers, so maybe he'll be able to," he said to Bobby.

Jeremy closed the cabin door, looked at Bobby, giving him a 'time to move on and I'm in charge' glance.

"Lead the way, Cochise," Bobby said, and moved out of the way.

Chapter 21

The two men made their way slowly along the deck. They were looking out for anyone who resembled a captain or anyone who may help with explaining where they were going. There was silence between the two. Jeremy was trying to fathom out what the pain and vivid images of Joanna meant, whilst Bobby didn't feel comfortable trying to make polite conversation.

Bobby had never been that sort of person. In fact, Bobby had been the sort of person who would easily talk with his fists rather than use his mouth.

They had reached the middle of the ship when they came upon a stairway leading up to the top deck. Jeremy looked at Bobby as if to say, 'shall we?'.

"What?" Bobby looked at Jeremy, none the wiser.

Jeremy had often worked with people like Bobby in the past, defending them in court, but whilst then, he was getting paid for his defending skills and patience, now was different. His tolerance was wearing thin. There were too many questions to be answered, and having to babysit this meat head at the same time was wearing thin. Jeremy breathed a sigh of frustration.

"Right, I'll go up shall I?" Jeremy said in a tone that was easily read as being that of someone who was extremely fed up.

"Hey! Who pulled your panties up your ass? I only asked what. I didn't need a reply like that. Keep coming out with shit like that and me and you are going to have to have more than words. Understand lawyer? I don't give a shit who you are. You *will* give me respect."

Bobby squared up to Jeremy with fire in his eyes.

Jeremy was in no mood for idiots like Bobby, and especially on a ship going god knows where and that he couldn't even say how he even boarded the vessel. Jeremy bit his lip and gave a limp apology.

"I'm only saying, and if I offended you, then I didn't mean to. There's way too many questions left unanswered and I am getting a little frustrated with everything that's going on," Jeremy said, trying to make as brief as eye contact as possible. "You coming up with me?"

Bobby looked at the stairs and back at Jeremy.

"Sure."

It was then Bobby's turn to collapse. A sudden attack of heat and the sensation of sweat trickling down his neck, a sharp pain at the back of the head, sent Bobby to his knees.

"Goddammit!" he said as he cradled the back of his head with his right hand. "What the shit?"

Jeremy was quicker to assist Bobby than Bobby was to assist him when his pain had arrived, and bent down to help.

"You OK?" he said as he helped Bobby up.

"Holy shit. That stings," Bobby said as he rubbed the back of his head.

Jeremy knew Bobby's visions were also becoming more vivid as the pain increased.

"Can I just ask? Did you see anything? I mean, any images in your head?"

"Jesus! Let me get up first, will you?" Bobby said, scowling at his helper.

Jeremy held back his frustration and helped Bobby to his feet. After a moment's recovery, Jeremy was back on with his questioning.

"So? Did you see any images? I need to push you on this, as it could be important," Jeremy asked, urging him for a reply.

Bobby rubbed the back of his head and winced at the pain whilst trying to recall his images.

"Yes, now you mention it, yes I saw stuff. I saw my pickup parked on a dark road. Think it might have been Alabama River Parkway as it wasn't lit and I recognise the bend in the road with Gun Island Chute to my right. It was raining and there was another car. Shit knows what had happened, but I was getting wet. I was out of my pickup. Think I slapped some dickweed for pulling out in front of me. Then I'm hot and sweating like a whore who's hired by her daddy. Know what I'm saying?"

Bobby continued rubbing the back of his head and looked out at the ripples on the sea.

"Thing is, lawyer, these are just images in my head. I don't remember this ever happening, so what the hell does that mean?"

Jeremy felt the same way about his thoughts. Vivid, but no way could they be real. Surely he would have remembered them. And if they were real, then what was that pain he had suffered? Heart attack? Couldn't be. He was fit and kept himself healthy. Although, he knew of football players who had collapsed on the field whilst playing. Maybe he was having a heart attack, but if so, then why couldn't he remember anything from then? Especially getting on board this yacht and where he was heading to?

"Well...? Anything?" Bobby interrupted Jeremy's thoughts.

"Nothing at the moment."

"Goddamn waste of time talking to you. What the hell you ask all these questions for and don't come back with any solutions. Jesus, man! You get paid millions, but you can't come out with any answers. What sort of lawyer are you anyways?"

Jeremy was on the verge of exploding and Bobby was his target, however his logical side sensed there was no point in doing so as he needed to find answers and not make things any worse than they already were.

"Look, I'm going up. Are you coming or what?" Jeremy said, looking at the stairway. "There may be some answers up there. You never know, the goddamned captain may be there."

Jeremy didn't wait for Bobby to answer and climbed the metal stairway.

"Hold on there, Cochise. I'm coming too. If there is anything to find, I want to be there too," Bobby said as he followed up the stairs.

Moments later, the two men were on the top deck and surveying their surroundings. The moon had risen more but was still on the wrong side if Manny was to be believed at to the direction they were travelling in.

It was a cloudless night, the moon shining brightly, reflecting off the ripples of the water. With not a star in the sky, and only the moon to light the horizon, the two men scoured the area for any land markings or anything that could tell them where they were. Nothing but water all around the ship.

"Hey lawyer. Is that where the captain is?" Bobby pointed to a door to their left.

On the top of the vessel was the bridge. The outside looked just as luxurious as they could see through the windows. Inside was a bank of switches, lights, and pulleys with what looked like some form of radio. Neither man could see anyone inside.

"Let's go see if we can find any maps or anything that could tell us our destination," Jeremy said, walking towards the door.

Chapter 22

Before entering, Jeremy looked through the window once more to see if anyone was inside that they had not initially seen. Nothing. A quick scan around the top deck to make sure there was no one there too, and Jeremy opened the door and went inside.

"What the hell is going on, lawyer?" Bobby said in awe as he followed Jeremy inside the bridge.

Inside the bridge was nothing but old wood panels, similar to those from an ancient gondola. Not a panel of switches or pulleys, no radio, just an open space. Even the walls and windows had disappeared and the two men could see an unfamiliar landscape, different from the one they had just seen outside the bridge. Both men stood motionless, trying to come to terms with what they were seeing.

The ship was sailing down what looked like a river, with boulders jutting out of the water on both sides. A short distance away appeared enormous cliff-like facades flanking the ship.

They could no longer see the moon, as the rocky walls continued up further and over the vessel, creating a tunnel that enveloped the ship. Apart from old wood, the only other things to be seen were lanterns.

On the front of the vessel was an old candle-lit lantern, gently illuminating the rocky waters ahead. In the distance, another light. This was larger than the ship's lantern, more like a beach beacon. It stood prominently on a small jetty, its flames guiding their way.

"I don't freaking believe this, lawyer. What the hell is going on?" Bobby said, gazing ahead.

Jeremy had no answer. He knew what he could see and there was no way that the yacht had been an illusion; he had felt its reality. The seats in the lounge, the sun loungers on the lower decks, even his favourite whisky. Everything was real.

"I'm going to have a look down at the front and see this light. I don't believe a tub like this would have a light like that at the front, and to be honest with you, lawyer, I'm getting a little pissed with all this shit. It ain't right, and I'm going to find out what the hell is happening."

Bobby left Jeremy staring out at the beacon that seemed only a mile or so away. Where did it come from and why didn't they see that and the cliff walls whilst they were previously outside? Fear crept into Jeremy's mind. This was a very weird dream or something just as strange. There was no way this could be real unless he had gone insane, and he didn't feel that way, so what was happening? Jeremy controlled his panic as it rose from deep inside.

"Get it together," he said to himself. "There's got to be an explanation for all this. But what that may be, I really don't know!"

Bobby had made his way to the bow and looked up at where the lantern should have been. The yacht was back, with no rotting damp wood, just a gleaming ship, made for billionaires. Jeremy looked down at

Bobby as he peered over the bow of the old boat, and for a moment, he just stayed there.

"Lawyer! Come down here! You gotta see this shit! This is gonna freak you out!" Bobby shouted, beckoning as he did.

Jeremy ran out of the bridge and back onto a pristine yacht. Nearly falling down the flight of stairs, he ran over to where Bobby was, who was now looking over the bow again.

"What? What is it?" Jeremy said, panting.

Without looking up, Bobby replied.

"Man, you will not believe this shit."

Jeremy joined Bobby and looked over the edge of the bow.

"This can't be. It's impossible," Jeremy said as he stared at the waves below.

Chapter 23

'How was this possible?' They were going forward, yet the waves that should have been breaking on the bow appeared to be going in reverse. It looked like the bow of the ship was sucking the waves in and not pushing them to either side. Both men stared at the sight in disbelief.

"What is this shit?" Bobby said, fear rising in his voice. "I've never been on a ship of any sort, but I'm pretty sure that the waves should go in the other direction... Any answers, lawyer?" Bobby slowly looked up at Jeremy for an answer.

No explanation came.

"Excuse me, gentlemen. I must insist that you step away from the bow of the ship. It's not safe, so please...would you step away?"

Manny suddenly appeared, breaking the eerie silence. The waiter was close to the side deck which the two men had just come from with a tray in his right hand—a bottle of beer and a tumbler of whisky on it.

Swiftly turning, both startled men saw the crew member and instantly Bobby's anger flared. Running over to the waiter, Bobby lashed out at the man, sending the tray flying overboard and pinned the wide-eyed waiter against a nearby wall.

"Right, you little shit. You have a choice. You either tell me what the hell is happening here or I'm going to kick seven shades of shit out of you and, to be honest, I'm thinking of going straight to the second option."

Bobby's right forearm forced Manny against the wall putting pressure on his throat making it difficult for him to reply.

"Tell me now goddammit or so help me, I'll kick the living shit out of you!" Bobby shouted.

Jeremy watched as Bobby threatened the helpless waiter, who was trying to free himself from the clutches of the furious man. Jeremy's mind was a whirlwind of questions with no answers, as he stood and watched Bobby shout at the man and raise his left clenched fist to Manny's face.

"Sir, sir, please!" Manny croaked, trying to break free.

Bobby's fury overwhelmed him and he swung his fist back. Before he could launch it towards his victim's face, a tall, slender man dressed in a dark uniform appeared and took hold of Bobby's left forearm, preventing the crashing blow. Jeremy watched the appearance on Bobby's face change from one of rage to one of realisation and then of absolute fear, all in a matter of seconds. The tall man never said a word but just looked at Bobby, who was now visibly trembling and looking at Manny's rescuer.

"No! No! That's bullshit!" Bobby shouted as he kept his gaze on the tall man and backed away from the waiter.

The stranger released the grip from Bobby's arm. With a look of dread that Jeremy had only seen once before in his life, Bobby turned to face Jeremy.

As a young lawyer, he had defended a man who was found guilty and had been on death row. The message Jeremy had seen on Bobby's face was exactly the one he had seen on his client, as the guards had placed him in the electric chair just before they placed the hood on him and they pulled the switch.

Whatever this man had done to Bobby was something so profound that it had caused this violent redneck to fear for his life. As soon as he could, Bobby flashed a fearful glance over to Jeremy and darted off down the side of the ship, out of sight, leaving Jeremy, Manny, and the tall officer alone.

Jeremy tried his best to come to his senses. With everything that was occurring he approached the two men.

"Captain Obol, is it?" Jeremy said with a tremble in his voice.

"And you are Jeremy Leadstone. Once lawyer and owner of your own successful law firm," the captain said.

Picking up on the past tense comment, Jeremy stared at the tall man with a puzzling look.

"Once? Captain, your English is good but not brilliant. Much better than my Greek, I must admit, but not *once*. I still am," Jeremy corrected the captain.

The captain smiled and turned to Jeremy.

"And what makes you think I'm Greek?" he said calmly.

"Your name. Charon Obol. It's Greek, isn't it? Plus, one of your crew told me you were Greek," Jeremy said, seeking confirmation.

"It is Mr Leadstone. My name is Greek, but that's not to say that I am Greek. I am not. Neither does my English need correcting. I am fluent in every language," the Captain replied, smiling.

Jeremy's mind was taking on too much to work out what was being said to him.

"You must be wrong. I *am* a lawyer of a successful company, not *once*. Anyway, can you explain to me how on earth I got on board and where exactly are we going? I've no recollection of boarding this thing, and I say 'thing' as there's two ships in one here which is impossible, so whatever this *thing* is and whoever you are, can you tell me where we're going?"

Captain Obol smiled at Jeremy and relaxing his shoulders he approached him.

"So many questions. I can answer all of them if you wish, all in order I think would be best." Obol smiled a reassuring smile and turned to Manny. "Thank you, you can go now."

"Sir," Manny nodded, and hurried away.

Jeremy watched Manny retreat to the stern and turned his gaze back to the captain.

"Yes. I think in order would be good. So, how did I get on this godforsaken thing?"

Obol continued to smile at Jeremy and came closer to him, raising his right hand.

"If I may," he said to Jeremy as he reached out his index finger towards Jeremy's forehead.

Jeremy looked at the approaching captain's finger and then at the man himself, flinching briefly.

"I assure you I can't hurt you and you *do* want answers, don't you?" Obol said in a calming voice.

Jeremy relaxed and nodded slightly, allowing Obol to touch his forehead.

Chapter 24

"Hey honey, I'm home. Sorry I'm late, but you know how it is." Jeremy called out as he entered the hallway of his home, placing his briefcase on the floor, then removing his overcoat.

Jeremy placed his coat over his right arm and picked up his case. Walking across the marbled floor of his hall, he casually tossed the full-length coat over the bannister and made his way to the console in the middle of the hall where a crystal vase stood, displaying an expertly arranged bouquet of orchids. With his free hand, he picked up the mail from the table and sifted out all the junk mail, leaving just the one envelope in his hand.

"At last. It's about time," Jeremy said with a smile on his face as he recognised who the letter had come from.

"Honey? You here?" he called out, expecting to hear his wife reply in her usual way.

Jeremy wandered into his office off the left of the hall and placed his case on the floor by the side of his desk. He dropped the letter onto the desk.

As he walked over to the drinks cabinet, Jeremy sniffed his shirt collar and made sure that there was no lingering perfume on it from his 'late meeting'.

It was a good idea having wet wipes in his car so he could remove any trace of makeup from either his face or clothing prior to returning home. However, it was the perfume that could cause him a few issues, if Joanna ever noticed.

Not that she would ever say anything. She was onto a good thing, and so what if her husband had one or two little indiscretions? She wouldn't do anything. Jeremy made sure there was no lingering scent before he poured himself a large whisky.

"Joanna? You upstairs?" Jeremy called out after taking a huge gulp of the warming liquid.

A brief scan of the lounge and kitchen showed no signs of his wife, so Jeremy made his way up the stairs.

As he entered their bedroom, Joanna was standing by the bed, staring at her husband. In her hand was an A4 manila envelope that was shaking with her rage.

"Ah, you're here," Jeremy said, smiling as he placed the drink down on the top of a chest of drawers. "How's your day been?"

Jeremy sensed something was wrong, but played it naturally.

"Enlightening," came the curt reply. "Care to explain?"

Joanna threw the envelope onto the bed as Jeremy approached her to give her an obligatory peck on the cheek.

Halted in his tracks, Jeremy looked at the envelope then at his wife.

"What's that?" he said, sensing it wasn't anything good.

"Why don't you look and you tell me." Joanna's voice trembled, yet with a firmness that meant there was going to be a blazing row.

Jeremy quickly put his mind in gear, picked up the envelope and opened it, pulling out several coloured ten by eight-inch photographs. He sifted through each photograph, feigning close examination, when in reality he knew exactly what each photograph revealed.

The first couple of photographs were innocent enough, only having a drink at a bar with a beautiful auburn-haired woman. The rest becoming more explicit with each photograph as the photographer caught him and the woman naked in a hotel room. Jeremy tossed the photographs back on the bed and looked at his wife.

"What do you want me to say?" he said defiantly.

"Well, it's way past 'this isn't what it seems darling' that's for sure. You bastard. All these years, I have loved you. All I ever wanted was you and your love. I gave you everything. Even my loyalty. I suspected many times that things like this were going on, but now you're rubbing this in my face. I can't take this anymore. You're a total bastard. What have I done to deserve this? No, don't answer. You can't. Just tell me, who is this slut? Wasn't I enough? Well, obviously not, but why?" Joanna screamed as tears fell down her cheeks.

"Why? Because I can. All you wanted was to live the life I gave you. And the price of all this was to leave me to do what I want. Now you want it all and for me to stop? Not a chance. You want a divorce then that's fine, just remember the prenup you signed. Nothing. You get nothing. You want to leave all this? The cars, the jewellery, the clothing, the lifestyle? All gone. Now. Stop being a prissy little bitch and be thankful I give you the life you have."

Jeremy was in no mood for his 'little wife' to be angry with him after what he had provided her with.

Joanna glared at him with a rage he had never seen before.

"So what you going to do, Joanna? Tell me. What?" Jeremy said as he stared into her tear-filled, enraged eyes.

As Jeremy turned to walk back to his whisky, Joanna let out a scream of rage choked by tears. With his back to Joanna and taking only a couple of paces, a masked figure appeared from the en-suite behind him and raised his right hand, pointing the barrel of a gun at his back. A loud crack, and Jeremy jerked forward with a jolt and a searing pain to his chest. His white shirt suddenly exploded as the bullet exited his chest, tearing a hole in his heart and covering his shirt with crimson. Jeremy fell to his knees, and before he could grab his chest, he was dying, falling face down on the plush carpet, staining it with his blood.

Clive Denby—removing his balaclava—walked over to the limp body oozing life and stared into the fading eyes of his competition.

"My turn now," Clive muttered to the dying body on the carpet.

Joanna burst into tears, partly from relief that her nightmare had ended and partly because her one and only love was dying.

Clive turned and walked over to the sobbing woman and, placing an arm around her, consoled her for a moment before turning her to look him in his face.

"I appreciate how difficult this must be, but remember the plan."

Clive removed a roll of tape from his jacket pocket. Whilst still crying, Joanna turned and placed both hands behind her back.

"I know. An unknown masked man entered our home and tied me up, claiming to be a father of a victim of a defendant that Jeremy had freed from court," Joanna sobbed. "The attacker claimed he was seeking retribution for his daughter. Jeremy comes home, and he shoots him and makes off. I break free and call the police.

I describe the man as Jeremy's size, which is easy to remember so the police cannot trip me up and I back pedal." She looked over at her now dead husband, his wound still oozing blood. "I never saw his face, and he just left me tied up. A month after the police close the case with no suspects, I then sell Jeremy's law firm to the second largest law firm in the country; Denby Law Incorporated. Not wanting anything to do with the firm anymore, I sell it for ninety percent of its value, making it look like you've got a good deal.

I get rid of my bastard husband without the prenup agreement coming into play. Yes, I think I've got it. Just make sure you do your bit and the police don't start asking anymore questions."

Joanna sat down on a dressing chair near to Jeremy's body and looked at her husband.

"Yes, you've got that alright. I'll stick to my side of the bargain. Just don't rip me off and we'll both come out of this on top."

Clive crouched down in front of Joanna and looked into her eyes.

"Are you sure about this?"

"Of course I'm sure. Just get it over with quickly, will you?" Joanna said, shuffling into a comfortable position on the chair.

Clive stood up and delivered a crashing blow to Joanna's jaw, sending her off the chair and landing next to the bed.

"I'm sorry," he whispered and ran out of the bedroom, down the stairs and calmly out of the Leadstone residence as if nothing had happened.

Joanna lay on the floor looking at her dead husband and his blood that had soaked the carpet they had just bought.

"You bastard. All you ever wanted was more. More wealth, larger company, and more than I could ever give you. You selfish bastard."

***

Jeremy came to as Charon Obol removed the finger from his forehead. A look of disbelief spread across Jeremy's face as he stared into the soulless eyes of the captain.

"I don't understand," he said and broke his stare with Charon. "I mean, it explains my visions and the pain in my chest, but Jo wouldn't have done that. Even if she did, then how would that explain me being here?"

"Think about it, Mr Leadstone. Your images and the pain you felt actually happened. You wake up here on my ship not knowing how you got here or where you're going. Where do you think you are? Are you alive? Is this a dream? Come on, Mr Leadstone, you're an intelligent man. Think. What happened to you, and where are you now?"

Jeremy tried to think of every possibility. Each ended with the same conclusion. It couldn't be. Surely, this must be a dream. A very weird, hyper-realistic dream. Nothing made sense other than he was dead.

"Are you telling me I'm—" Jeremy started.

"You and everyone else on my boat, Mr Leadstone," Charon said.

"How come it was only me who thought that something was wrong? The others seemed to be OK with being here."

Jeremy looked around the deck hoping he may see someone, anyone, who could tell him that this was one of those TV prank programmes that get aired on several cable channels.

"You and Mr Bobby Johnson," Charon corrected him. "Everyone else saw their ending taking shape. It was only you and Bobby who didn't. You were shot in the back, as you now know, and a woman who was protecting her husband delivered a deadly blow to the back of Mr Johnson's head.

Mr Johnson was an angry man who picked on a driver on a dark road. Whilst he beat on the driver, his wife picked up a tyre iron from the back of their pickup and hit her husband's attacker over the back of his head, killing him instantly.

Your acquaintance, Miss Christine Sommers? Her latest surgery didn't go according to plan. During her gym session, one of her implants that had a liquid that should not have been there burst, and well, now she's here.

And Mr Stephen Hibbert? Maybe he should not have trusted his ex-partner's wife. You were first met by Marcus Hall. He was in his apartment when the fire alarm went off. He tried, like everyone else, to get out, but because of his size, he tripped as he went down the stairs. The rest of the occupants didn't care who they trampled on as they tried to escape. All he could feel was the air being squeezed from his chest by the many feet standing on him. I could go on with every other passenger if you like."

Jeremy's head reeled with the revelation of his current situation.

"And everything that was different on the ship?" Jeremy's voice quivered.

"The River Styx is a strange place and as much as I try to make it a comfortable journey, there are some things that give you clues to where you are. You were right about the moon. It was rising in the wrong half of the sky and whilst I can give my boat the appearance of a nice yacht, there are areas I don't expect you to visit.

You went where you shouldn't have and noticed the real vessel. The man in the lounge whom Mr Hibbert assaulted, would never die. How could he when he was already deceased? No, we just placed a loop and made it normal for everyone. Everyone but you and Miss Somers. I had to involve her as she was with you, and you would have just convinced her what really happened. So I could not see the point in making her think otherwise."

"What about the guy who jumped overboard?" Jeremy asked.

"Ah, now he, too, died without knowing. He found out what was happening and where we're going. He tried to escape his destiny by leaving the ship. Not the brightest idea." Charon said.

"There was no splash or body when I looked."

"There wouldn't be Mr Leadstone. The leviathan made sure of that. I believe you were told that these are dangerous waters and to stay away from the edge of the ship. I'm afraid Mr Greenbaum jumped from the frying pan into the furnace."

"You mean the fire?"

"No, Mr Leadstone. The leviathan is much worse than where you're going."

Jeremy paused and thought. Dead, River Styx, Leviathan. There was only one place this ship was heading. He could now see the ship and captain for what and who they were.

"You're the—"

"I prefer Charon to 'ferryman'. And yes, you're right about the destination before you say."

Jeremy's stomach sank, knowing that where they were about to land was a place, he had only seen in films and read in books.

"Before you say it, it is real, and it is right. Your sin, Mr Leadstone, was greed. Miss Sommers, pride, Mr Johnson, wrath. I could tell you the others, but it makes no difference." Charon looked up and smiled. "We're here now."

The ship slowly came to a halt, brushing up gently against the wooden jetty. The flickering flame from the burning beacon on the end of the pier cast light and shadows on the boat like dancing demons.

The stench of hopelessness mixed with the wails of agony made Jeremy want to collapse, but something held him up. He looked overboard at the foreboding scenery that welcomed him with open arms. The air was thick with fear, much worse than Jeremy could ever imagine.

Moments later, hearing clambering footsteps, every one of the unaware souls appeared at the front of the ship. Christine Sommers was the first to appear with Stephen by her side, eager to disembark.

"Monaco! I recognise that brasserie anywhere!" Christine shouted out as she ran towards the exit ramp.

Stephen trotted after her with not as much excitement, but seeing that Jeremy was standing with a smartly dressed man, whom he thought would have been the captain, flaunted the notion that he was with her.

Jeremy looked at the faces of everyone heading for the ramp with joyous smiles. Only he could see the reality of where they were and the vessel they were leaving.

"Why do they not see? Monaco? How've you done that?" Jeremy asked as he looked at Charon.

"Oh, they'll change their minds when they set foot on land. The illusion only works on here. Only you can see because I gave you the ability. You knew something was wrong, and I decided not to fool you. Your friend Mr Johnson, however, not so smart and took a different option. The one with the leviathan. I tried to tell him, but he was a little headstrong."

Jeremy was listening to what was being said, but watched as everyone queued to leave. One of the crew members was standing by the ramp onto the jetty with a cap in his hand as everyone dug into their pockets and pulled out coins. It surprised some that they had such a thing, but did not hesitate to hand over the required sum of money for the journey.

"It all makes sense now. Your name, Charon Obol. It's just Charon, isn't it? Obol was the coin given to you, and the ship the Pendentes was the name of your boat. All from Greek mythology." Jeremy muttered.

"Well, I wouldn't say it was a myth, but yes, you are correct." Charon replied.

Jeremy deftly padded his trouser pockets in the hope of not finding a coin. With relief, he smiled and looked at Charon.

"And what if you don't pay the ferryman? What happens then? You can't drop people off without payment, can you?" Jeremy said defiantly.

Charon looked at the passengers handing over the required payments and sighed.

"This is true Mr Leadstone. I do not transport anyone without payment."

"Well, I wonder what you would do with me?" Jeremy said with a wry smile.

Charon turned to Jeremy with eyes that sent a shiver into his very soul.

"But, Mr Leadstone, your payment had already been made," Charon replied.

It startled Jeremy at the revelation. Who would make such a payment in advance?

"But I haven't handed over any such payment, not even for any of the drinks. What do you mean, you've been paid?" his voice trembled.

"His Infernal Majesty. He's been waiting for you. He paid for your journey himself. Apparently, you are his favourite deadly sin." Charon explained.

Jeremy's knees felt weak at the information, and the pit of his stomach felt a fear he had never experienced before.

"His infernal majesty? You mean the Devil, don't you?" Jeremy could feel the tidal wave of panic rising. "He paid for my journey. His favourite deadly sin? What have I committed?" Jeremy said, with fear in every word.

"Why, greed, Mr Leadstone. Lucifer's favourite sin is greed. And you, Mr Leadstone, have led your life with a passion for such. Everything you have ever done has been purely for greed. You even signed a contract—"

"I would never sign a contract with the Devil," Jeremy interrupted. "Never with the Devil."

"Oh, but you did, Mr Leadstone. He was your first major client who had your services as a retainer when you started your law firm. Surely you read the contract. You were a lawyer. You must have read in its entirety before signing."

Jeremy recalled the meeting with a certain CEO of Bringer Light and Information Corporation. The contract had the words 'retainer' and 'yearly fee' plus a figure which included several numbers just after a dollar sign. Hungry for such a contract, he had not bothered to read the rest, as all he could see was the money that would roll in every year, without fail.

Jeremy wracked his brain to remember everything about the meeting where he had signed his life away.

'The CEO was a stunning woman whose looks were beyond anything he had seen before...What was her name..? Lucy! Lucy, Lucifer. The epitome of a wolf in sheep's clothing.' Jeremy realised they had conned him purely down to his greed and an expert distraction method.

"The bringer of light. Lucifer. Goddammit," Jeremy muttered, knowing he had been beaten.

"Oh, the irony, Mr Leadstone. Anyway, everyone has now left now, so I'll bid you goodbye—"

"And if I refuse to leave?" Jeremy interrupted.

In a blink of an eye, Charon replied.

"Then I shall have to take you off myself."

Charon raised his hand and took hold of Jeremy's elbow. There was no gust of wind, no dizziness to signify any form of movement, but the ground under Jeremy's feet had a sudden difference. He was now on land and could see the Pendentes over the shoulder of its captain.

"I'm sorry, but you really don't have a say in this, Mr Leadstone," Charon said gently but firmly, with no room for discussion.

As he patted Jeremy's shoulder, Charon turned to board what now was a long gondola-style boat, a small candlelit lantern at the bow.

Jeremy watched as the ferryman took his leave. The shock of what was happening drowned out the shouts and screams of the other passengers, who now could see exactly where they were standing.

The old bearded man, dressed in a linen hooded cloak, boarded his empty boat, and picked up a single long oar. Charon placed the oar in the River Styx at the rear of the boat and manoeuvred away from the jetty.

The other passengers were screaming and huddled together like frightened sheep as Jeremy Leadstone, once owner of what was the largest law company in America, watched Charon 'The Ferryman' row away on the Pendentes into the darkness for another journey.

As the lantern of the boat faded into the darkness, the stench of sulphur and an overwhelming fear enveloped Jeremy. He turned to see the rest of the group, hoping to feel a little security in numbers.

Everyone had disappeared; Christine, Stephen, Bobby, everyone.

Jeremy scanned the area to see if they had moved to a safer place or if, by some infinitesimal chance, someone rescued them from this hellish nightmare. Nothing. The feeling of being alone in a place so depraved and evil eventually took over Jeremy, and he collapsed to his knees. No amount of regret or remorse could help him escape his destiny.

"Please God. Help me. Please, I'm begging you. Take me. Please don't leave me here," he begged, as tears of panic and fear flowed down his cheeks.

Something inside of this broken man suddenly made him stop and look up. Where all the frightened passengers once stood was a single figure. Blacker than the blackest night. A depth of evil far greater than any living soul could imagine. No discernible size or shape, just black, with an imperceptible smile that would freeze the hottest flame and piercing flame red eyes, ready to cauterise his soul.

"God can't help you here, Jeremy Leadstone."

ACKNOWLEDGEMENTS

I cannot express enough thanks to Caro Simpson, my editor and proofreader, for making this book a diamond from the rough. Having an idea in your head and words written down doesn't make for an excellent book. It takes someone to take the raw materials and make them into something worth having. Thanks a million.

Finally, to my loving and supportive wife, Caroline, and my wonderful son, Kris: my deepest gratitude. Your encouragement, ability to keeping me young, and at times totally bewildered are very much appreciated. It has been a great journey made more enjoyable by you two. My heartfelt thanks and eternal love to you both.

Books by M.J. Todd

The Sinkhole Chronicles series - Satire
The Prodigal Vampire
Gary's Inferno

The Night Boat – Suspense Thriller Mystery

Sinkhole Chronicles Merchandise

www.redbubble.com/people/MJ-Todd/shop

All merchandise designed by Shadow2403.
Check out his website on
www.redbubble.com/people/Shadow2403/shop

Editor and Proofreader

Caro Simpson
Email: csimpsoneditor@gmail.com

Printed in Great Britain
by Amazon